I0735072

MARY CRAWFORD

Paths NOT Taken

HIDDEN BEAUTY BOOK 8

Copyright

ISBN: 978-1-945637-47-6

Cover by Covers Unbound

HIDDEN BEAUTY SERIES

Until the Stars Fall from the Sky

So the Heart Can Dance

Joy and Tiers

Love Naturally

Love Seasoned

Love Claimed

If You Knew Me (and other silent musings) (novella)

Jude's Song

The Price of Freedom (novella)

Paths Not Taken

Dreams Change (novella)

Heart Wish (100% charity release)

Tempting Fate

The Letter

The Power of Will

Hidden Hearts Series

Identity of the Heart

Sheltered Hearts

Hearts of Jade

Port in the Storm (novella)

Love is More Than Skin Deep

Tough

Rectify

Pieces (a crossover novel)

Hearts Set Free

Freedom (a crossover novel)

The Long Road to Love (novella)

Love and Injustice (Protection Unit)

Out of Thin Air (Protection Unit)

Soul Scars (Protection Unit)

OTHER WORKS:

The Power of Dictation

Use Your Voice

An Everyday Guide to Scrivener 3 for Mac

Vision of the Heart

DEDICATION

Each person must
choose their own path
— for no single path goes
to all destinations.

This book is dedicated to
those who are brave enough
to forge their own
path without fear.

CHAPTER ONE

JORDAN

"Jordan!" my boss, Mishka, bellows the second my pathetic egg salad sandwich hits my lips. It's all I can do not to let a few cuss words fly. I haven't even had a moment to eat, and it's three thirty in the afternoon. If I don't eat soon, I'm going to pass out. It's as simple as that. When I don't answer immediately, she yells again, "Jordan, are you even listening? I need you."

I take a moment to draw in a deep breath and choke down a couple of quick bites of my sandwich. I grimace and wash it down with stale, cold coffee. For the four thousand three hundred and fifty-seventh time today, I wonder why I even bothered to go to college.

I grab a steno pad and make my way to Mishka's office. Before I enter the door, I try unsuccessfully to smooth out the wrinkles from my silk skirt. This fabric is stunning to look at, but it does have a down side or two. Schooling my face into a neutral expression, I inch into her office and sit on her designer couch. Mishka's office is cold, white and astute like the entire studio. It's as if she tries to intimidate clients with her artistic sensibility.

"Something I can do for you?" I cross my legs and balance my notebook on my knee. I try not to smirk as I take in Mishka's ensemble. Today, she looks as if she wrapped herself in bed sheets and added a turban with artificial flowers woven into it.

She scowls. "Did you order the lanyards for our upcoming show? I haven't heard anything from the printer."

I swallow a sigh. "No, I have not heard from them. Then again, I wouldn't expect to since we just turned the job in yesterday. Like I tried to tell you the other day, it's Niko's job to monitor all that stuff for you. You hired me to be a clothing designer."

Mishka looks down her nose at me and glares. "You will be a designer when I say you are a designer. Otherwise, you just work for me and you'll do whatever I tell you to do."

I stiffen and bite my lip. "Exactly how long do I need to pay my dues? I have been serving as your lackey for more years than I'd like to admit. It seems you've forgotten, I'm qualified to do more."

Mishka waves me away. "I decide who is promoted and who is not. You may go now. Obviously, you are no help to me. Go do whatever it is you do at your desk."

Gritting my teeth, I nod. "Sorry I couldn't help you," I reply stiffly. I bite the inside of my cheek to avoid saying more.

Slamming the tablet of paper down on my desk, I stalk off to the break room in search of hot coffee. The coffee isn't even done brewing yet when the bell at my desk rings. *Really? I wonder what she wants now?*

Rolling my shoulders and shaking out my fingers in an effort to calm down, I try to shed my anger before I have to face her again. Today has already been hellaciously long, and it's not close to over yet.

When I walk out of the break room, I come to an abrupt halt, my way barred by a tall, wide-shouldered man who looks as surprised as I am. Of course, that could be because I ran straight into the middle of his chest. My mouth starts to water a little. We often work with the very definition of handsome around here, but the professional models have nothing on this guy.

When I look up into his eyes, he asks me in a tired voice, "Are you someone who can make some decisions around here?"

His question was benign and probably not meant to be loaded. Yet, his simple question gets at the crux of my problem working for Mishka. When I first started working here, I had a certain degree of autonomy, but over the past few months, she's started to micromanage everything I do. Her actions have effectively stripped me of all my decision-making power.

Slinking back to my desk, I pull out the sign-in sheet. "I am just a minion, but I can get you to someone who makes decisions. Can you tell me why you're here?"

"That's an excellent question. I mean, do I look like the kind of guy who belongs in a foo-foo designer place?"

I have to bite my tongue because there are so many things I could say about this man's appearance and how beautifully clothes would hang on him. If I were to verbalize what's happening in my overactive imagination at the moment, things could get awkward in a hurry.

"I think it's *loco*, but my promotion team wanted me to do it to gain fans across multiple platforms, so here I am."

"Okay, we've established you actually intend to be at Mishka Unlimited. That's a good start. Can I get your name?"

"I knew it. I figured I'd be the only guy who has ever set foot in a place like this. Randall must be punking me," the guy says, looking around the store as if he's searching for hidden cameras.

I probably should be offended by the inherent disdain for my whole occupation, but he looks so uncomfortable I don't have the heart to be mad at him. "Take a deep breath." I can't keep my bemused smile tamed. "This isn't a torture chamber; we just make clothes for people."

"I think I would prefer torture. There isn't anything I hate more than clothes shopping."

I study him for a moment. "With your height and shoulder width, I bet it's a pain. Have you considered having your clothes made custom?"

"I don't care enough about my clothes to do anything like that. Whatever fits, works for me."

I click my tongue at him. "More's the pity. Your body is designed to wear clothes — great clothes."

The guy checks his watch impatiently as he runs his hand through his artfully shaggy hair. "If it's all the same to you, can you round up the decision-maker? I'm running late for another appointment."

I bite the inside of my cheek. "I'd be happy to Mr. —"

He huffs at me. "I'm not sure why you need to know this, but my name is Cristiano Romero."

"I'm sure Mishka would like to know who she's meeting with. It's just common courtesy."

He reaches up and rubs his shoulder. "I apologize, I'm a little short on courtesy today."

I arch my eyebrow at him. "Isn't everyone? It's been one of those days."

He stops surveying the room and pins his gaze on me. "I'm sorry, I don't want your day to be going as crappy as mine."

I turn back to my desk and hit my intercom button to announce his arrival. "Let me see what I can do to expedite this for you," I comment as I wait for an answer.

Without warning, Mishka's voice comes through the intercom. Much to my mortification, the intercom is set on speaker. Our guest can hear every word.

"Are you incompetent or just plain stupid, Jordan Shepherd?" I'm completely frozen with my hand hovering over the intercom button. As soon as I hear Mishka's condescending tone. I know this won't go well. "You know I'm working on my latest collection. Oh wait, you're not a real designer so you couldn't possibly know what it's like."

I roll my eyes and try to ignore the fact that my boss just ripped me to shreds in front of a stranger. Suddenly

I reach my limit. It's been months in the making, but once I start speaking words erupt like volcanic debris. "With all due respect, Mishka, there would be no coattails without the things I've done — work which you'll be doing yourself because I'm done. I've worked too hard to get an education and experience to be treated worse than dirt. Go find yourself another victim because I'm finished."

"What about your two-weeks' notice?" she splutters.

"I'm gonna skip the whole notice thing. You owe me about nine weeks of vacation pay, anyway."

"How do you figure I owe you that much time?"

"It's easy. My contract says I get three weeks of vacation time every year. The only time I've taken any was when my mom had cancer. Even if you subtract my time off, you still owe me for more than two months' worth of vacation. Just tell the courier service to deliver my check because I'll be at home packing."

"I made you in this business, I will take you down," she blusters.

"I can't go much lower than I am already. If you have the power to take me down even further, I guess it's up to you to decide whether it's worth the effort. At this point, I don't care."

"You haven't heard the last of this. I'm going to have my lawyer go through our contract with a fine-tooth comb to make sure you don't owe me anything."

I can't bring myself to look over to Mishka's client. I am too humiliated. As I struggle to contain my embarrassment, I take the pen from behind my ear and march to Mishka's office and throw the pen down on her austere desk.

"Here, this is all I have that belongs to Mishka Unlimited," I declare. "Use it in good health."

"Just so you know, all the designs you've been working on belong to me."

"I guess it's a lucky thing for me you haven't allowed me to do any design work — even though it's what you hired me for. I have to say I liked you better when I knew you as Elouise Hadley. The person I met way back then wouldn't treat me this way. I hope you find her again." Emotion drips from my voice.

"I told you never to say my name again. I have become Mishka."

"Well, good for you." I stand up abruptly. "You have someone waiting for you." I dig my keychain out of my purse and take my office keys off my key fob. "I'd like to say it's been nice working for you, but it hasn't."

Before she can say a word, I turn on my heel and stride from the office. I stop to grab a couple of personal photos off my desk. I unlock my drawer and pull out my purse and stick the pictures in it. I'm blinking back tears and struggling to breathe as adrenaline courses through my body.

Cristiano clears his throat. "Well, this is awkward. It's an official; Jordan Shepherd, you're having a worse day than me."

In that moment, I want to fall through the floor and disappear. Instead, I stiffen my spine and walk out the door as if all of this kind of stuff happens every day.

⸺•⸺

"Jordie, take a deep breath. You're going to make yourself sick. I'm sure things will work out," my brother says as he adjusts his webcam.

"That's your considered medical opinion? How in the world is everything going to be okay? I just blew up my entire life." I choke back a sob. I've been crying for so long my ribs hurt. I barely made it home before I was overcome with tears and white-hot anger. I'm furious at myself for allowing the situation to get completely out of control. It seemed like a great idea at the time, but now I'm feeling lost.

Jaxson brings my attention back to him. "For one thing, you've been under-appreciated in your job for years. You are far more talented than Mishka gave you credit for. Look at this as an opportunity to stretch your wings and fly a little."

Feeling defeated, I wipe tears from my face. "I don't even know if I remember how to fly and I definitely don't want to fly all by myself in New York. What if she does have the power to completely blackball me?"

My brother shrugs. "It's also possible she was merely talking smack. If you don't want to be in New York, come back home. We miss you."

I smile at his invitation, but sigh as I consider the ramifications. "I don't really want to come home with my tail between my legs. I never did make it big like I had planned to."

Jaxson shakes his head. "You wouldn't be the first

person whose plans didn't work out exactly how you thought they would. That doesn't mean you have to come back feeling like a failure."

"Says you, *Dr. Shepherd.* You don't ever let anyone down."

My brother is like the golden child who can never do wrong.

Jaxson's brows come together, and his smile turns to a frown. "I think you have a short memory. I've let lots of people down, including my own daughter."

I give myself a mental kick. I should not have reminded him about the death of his first daughter. "I'm sorry Jax, I didn't mean to bring Jasmine in to it."

"You didn't. I did — to remind you that none of us are perfect. Come back home, Jordie. There are options for you here. Donda and Madison were impressed with the work you did to get Donda's story out to the media when she was trying to keep her stepdad in jail."

"I enjoyed working on her campaign, but it doesn't mean anyone else will take my resume seriously. I've basically been a glorified receptionist for years. Who's going to pay attention to my design chops or my journalism degree?"

"You're underselling yourself. I may be biased, but I know you'll be a rock star at whatever you decide to do."

"*Sheesh!* I'm too old for this crap. I'd be starting from scratch. Where do I even start?" I wipe my face off and collect myself. My panic level always skyrockets when catastrophic thoughts start tumbling around in my brain.

My sister-in-law, Donda walks into the frame. "I can

tell you from personal experience, it is not too late to start over. I started Claim Your Space after a parade of failures. All my work is finally paying off."

"Well, it should. You are insanely talented."

"So are you. Trust me, if someone treats you like that Mishka chick did, they don't deserve all your tears. Come get to know your niece. We'll get you all fixed up," Donda offers with a sympathetic smile.

I rub the heels of my hands into my eyes and try to focus my thoughts. "You're right. There's nothing left for me here. Give me a few days to get everything wrapped up, and I'll be there." I attempt to smile. "I'll try not to be too obnoxious — but I have to let you know I like to listen to my music pretty loud."

"Hello — did you forget I have a teenage son? You don't know the meaning of the word loud. I can take whatever you dish out." Donda's open acceptance of me is stunning, given our past.

I swallow hard. "Thanks, Donda. I appreciate the chance to start over. Maybe this time I won't make such a mess of it."

CHAPTER TWO

CRISTIANO

I FEEL AWKWARD STANDING there with my arms out like some weird architectural sculpture. A woman with wild hair and a severe expression who introduced herself as Mishka insists whatever it is she is going to design will be the latest in runway fashion. I guess I have to take her word for it; I'm not the person to judge. I'd much rather be riding my bike through the mud or jumping over alligator pits. I don't think I'll ever get used to the dog-and-pony show which goes with my job now.

Without warning, my arm begins to drop. My shoulder socket is burning as if someone placed a burning piece of charcoal in it. As much as I hate to admit it, my last rotator cuff surgery didn't quite fix everything. Holding it up for this long is not a smart move on my part.

"I told you not to move!" The designer yanks my arm up, so it's parallel to the floor. "Can you not follow directions either?" When she twists my arm to get a better angle, the pain makes me sway a little.

Her sharp words bring back the exchange I heard earlier. I have to admit, I'm curious. I thought tensions between me and the network were high, but my dispute looks petty compared to what I witnessed today. After meeting Mishka and dealing with her for a few minutes, I have newfound sympathy for the mysterious Jordan Shepherd.

"Will this take much longer?" I growl as my shoulder seizes up again.

"If you don't stop moving, I'm never going to get this done. Some people are just so lazy."

I step off the dais and shrug out of the sample jacket and shirt so fast I barely have time to take a breath. My shoulder screams in pain. At this point, I'm so angry I strip off the pants too and stand there in my boxer shorts. "Guess what? I'm done with you too. You might be famous, and my boss might want to woo your fans — but it's not worth it to me to deal with people like you."

"How dare you say that? Do you have any idea who Mishka is?"

I roll my shoulder and shake my head. "Truthfully, I had no idea you even existed before this afternoon."

She narrows her eyes at me. "That's obvious; you dress like a peasant."

"Strangely, I'm okay with that," I retort as I snag my well-worn 501s from the floor.

"People like you don't deserve my clothes. You need a second-rate designer like Jordan Shepherd. She would probably suit you just fine."

"Not a bad idea. I'm sorry I wasted your time today

— but I am sorrier you wasted mine." I awkwardly put on my Levis and Henley shirt.

"I can ruin your reputation with one phone call."

"That's funny; you've used the same threat twice today. I've got news for you — I'm already a person of 'ill-repute' as the nuns in my old Catholic school would say. You can't do any damage to me I haven't already done to myself. You're welcome to take a run at it, if that's what makes you happy."

"Get out!" Mishka bellows as the veins in her temple bulge.

I fasten my belt and head toward the door. "That's the first thing you've said all day I agree with," I toss over my shoulder as I leave the shop.

———◆———

"You did what?" my executive producer, Rowden Randall, hisses at me when I break the news of my meeting with Mishka. "Do you realize this event could secure our contracts for the foreseeable future?"

I move the TENS unit from my shoulder to my knee while I balance the phone on my shoulder. I don't know why I bother. I think I'm too far gone for electrical nerve stimulation to make a whole heckuva lot of difference. My joints still feel like they're on fire.

"Honestly, I think changing the name of the show to something people could define and pronounce would help more than some high-class fashion show." I struggle to focus through the fog of pain.

"No can do. We've talked about this before. The

wife named the show, and she is a huge Scrabble fan. Xyresic is one of her favorite words."

"That's fine for Scrabble, but what does it have to do with the X-Games?"

"The answer is the same as it was the last time you asked this question. It means razor's edge. The title is perfect for our show; it's a great play on words."

I sigh. "Rowden, a play on words only works if people know the meaning of the words. In this case, I think our show title is over people's heads. Why not call it *The X-Games: Razor's Edge?*"

"Hey, that's good. I'll run it by Jubilee. I'd love to be in the permanent rotation for a change. Our air times and location in the cable lineup make it difficult for people to consistently find us." He sighs. "Unfortunately, that does not solve our wardrobe problem. This award is the real deal — our shot at making it into the big leagues. The network execs at ESPN will be expecting you to wear designer duds."

It's probably a good thing my boss can't see my eye roll. "Don't worry about it. I've got it covered. If you don't mind, I had an exhausting day today. If you want me to look halfway human on air, I need to go and get some rest."

"Whatever you do, don't embarrass us. This is not some place you could show up in board shorts and a T-shirt."

"I guess you think I have stupid written across my forehead." I blow out a frustrated breath. "I said I would get it sorted out and I will. Don't worry about it."

"I worry about you all the time. The way you present yourself reflects on my company's reputation. You can't look like some high-schooler on a spring break trip."

I don't even bother to hide my sigh. "If I buy a suit off the rack, I don't think it'll sway our fans one way or another. They watch our show to recap the action they weren't able to see in person. Fans don't tune in to see what I'm wearing."

"I keep telling you, Romero, in today's world, you can't just be an expert in your own field, you have to be a 'personality.' You have to think of the big picture. If you are dressed well enough, our company name will be re-tweeted everywhere."

"I've got this covered," I reply abruptly.

"Just so you know, that designer you blew off was our only option. I don't have other people lined up to make you presentable. You're on your own. Get it done." The phone abruptly goes dead.

Holding my cell phone in my hand like it's a brick, in the privacy of my living room, I can admit I have absolutely nothing covered. I don't know what compelled me to promise I could figure all this out — I don't know anything about the fashion business.

My mind conjures up the image of Jordan trying to keep control of her pride and her emotions this afternoon as she walked out of Mishka Unlimited. I guess it's time for some internet research; if Jordan worked for someone like Mishka, she probably has contact info somewhere on the web.

As I type Jordan Shepherd's name into my phone, I

am a little surprised by the images. She looked efficient and businesslike today, but the pictures on the Internet tell a different story. With her hair free, sultry makeup, and sexy clothes, she is off-the-chain glamorous. A real knockout.

After scrolling through several dozen pictures, I'm already jealous of the men she's hanging out with and all these pictures. Heck, if I could hang out with the likes of her, I would do red carpet events more often. It would almost be worth the effort to clean up.

I smile as I run across a video of her dancing to music by Aidan O'Brien. She looks at home on the dance floor. I don't know if I would ever be that comfortable, but it is a treat to be able to watch her dance with abandon. The happy person on this video is so different from the sad, dejected woman I met today.

I scroll through a few more pages before I find an old profile of hers on LinkedIn. Fortunately, it has a phone number and an email address which doesn't seem to be connected to Mishka Unlimited.

On a whim, I type in her phone number in the reverse directory. My stomach sinks to my feet as it pulls up her address. This is the outcome I wanted, but it's not safe. I hope I'm panicking unnecessarily because I am viewing the world through my fractured rose-colored glasses. I know I made a fool of myself today. It's like I injected myself with rude serum. If I just call her, chances are Jordan is not even going to speak to me. I know I probably wouldn't. I think this calls for a more strategic approach.

My heart pounds like it did when I went to my first dance in Junior High, flowers in my hand. What am I doing? I don't do stuff like this. Yet, here I am like an idiot. It'd probably serve me right if she slammed the door in my face. I am reevaluating my strategy of surprising her with a visit; this could go very badly. Guess it's too late for me to worry about it now.

A maintenance guy walks around me in the foyer while I'm waiting. He takes one look at the intercom light and shakes his head. "Good luck with that one, man. She has a loud growl and a big bite."

"Who, Jordan? I don't think so." Inexplicably, I feel the need to defend her from the random criticism.

"Watch yourself. She's a bit of a handful." He shrugs his shoulders and walks away.

If I was a bit apprehensive before, now I'm really nervous. All of a sudden, this seems like a universally bad idea.

Jordan peeks through a gap in her doorframe as she opens the door a scant couple of inches, leaving the chain locked.

"You? What are *you* doing here?" She shifts to get a better look at me through the small gap.

"I don't come to New York very often. Would you believe I need a tour guide?"

"I might believe you — except then you would have to explain how you tracked down my apartment." Her brow furrows as she sees the flowers in my hand. "I guess you can do that inside." She opens the door wider and steps out of the way.

I scoot past her, dragging a hand through my hair to get it out of my face. "It was frighteningly simple. You have a substantial footprint on the Internet."

"My job was very public, but I didn't think it would lead you to my front door."

"Granted, you weren't on Google Maps or anything, but it didn't take much effort to put the pieces together." I grimace. "You might want to do something about that — particularly if your former boss is as bent on revenge as it appears."

Jordan slumps against her banister on the stairs. "Please, don't remind me. It was one of the more unpleasant experiences in my life."

"Really? I have a different perspective. See, I've spent just a few minutes in the presence of the great Mishka. If she were no longer my boss, I'd be doing the happy dance while taking a victory lap."

"Oh, believe me," Jordan says with a laugh, "the part of me which isn't completely petrified and freaked out about not having a job for the first time since junior high school is having a heck of a party. Sadly, the other part of me is thinking ahead. I've got bills to pay, after all."

"That's actually one of the reasons I'm here. I came over today. I was in town, and I need to talk to you about an important project."

Jordan shoots me a confused look as she responds, "You want to speak to me? What kind of project is it?"

"You design clothing, right? Mishka told me about it."

Jordan lifts an eyebrow. "Oh, I bet she did. She probably went into excruciating detail about how horrible I am at it."

Embarrassed for her, I glance down at the floor before I comment, "There was a little bit of that going on, I won't lie. This is just a hunch — but I wonder if Mishka was so critical of you because she is jealous of your talent. At least, that's what it sounded like to me."

Jordan smirks. "I suppose it's possible — but I doubt it. Mishka is pretty confident in her own skills."

"I guess the question of the day is how confident are you in yours?"

"Depends on what you're talking about."

"Well, I find myself without a designer for a designer ball. So … I'd like to know if you could work with me."

"You want me to design something for you? Aren't you contracted with Mishka? I don't remember everything in my employment contract when I was hired, but I do know stealing clients from Mishka would get me into a world of trouble. She would have her lawyers on me like attack dogs."

I shrug. "Not an issue. I fired Ms. Silk."

Jordan's eyebrows lift. "Seriously? No one ever fires the great Mishka. I wish I could've been there to see it. It must've been hysterical."

"Well, let's just say that you're not the only person she has threatened to ruin today."

"At this point, I'm just over the whole thing. I'm ready to move on with my life. I'm moving to Oregon in a couple of weeks and put this whole coast and everything associated with it behind me."

"Well, that will make things a little more difficult." I frown.

"Make what more difficult?"

"I was serious. I have to do this charity gig for my company. According to my executive producer, this event will put us on the map. He also told me I'm not allowed to show up wearing shorts and a T-shirt. So, I need some designer clothes."

"How do you know you'll like my style? Do you even know what I do?"

"I guess I don't. You had the good sense to quit your job this week. You are at least a little bit sane."

"I don't know, the jury is still out. We'll see what happens when I get to Oregon."

"Of all the states, why Oregon?"

"My family is there. I was all alone here in New York City. Now, I am returning home feeling like a colossal failure."

"Look, I know I was only a casual bystander, but it seems to me you were faced with an untenable situation and had to make hard choices. Based on what I saw the other day, I don't disagree with the decision you made. If I were in your shoes, I probably would've done the same thing."

Jordan lets out a short laugh. "That's nice … but you have no idea what chaos this has started in my life."

"I can imagine it probably opened up some soul-searching opportunities. All big risks do."

"Big risk? Don't you mean harebrained and impulsive?"

"Sometimes, we do things for self-preservation. I've had to go down that road before. It's scary, but not impossible."

"I appreciate the pep talk, but there's no way around the fact that my life sucks right now."

"I'm sorry things are so rough. I have a plan which might help both of us. I really do want to hire you to make my clothes for this event. I don't want to embarrass my boss or look like I don't fit in."

Jordan looks up at me. "I hate to break it to you, but there isn't much I can do to make you fit in. You are the kind of guy who is made to stand out."

My disappointment must have shown on my face because she quickly adds, "Don't worry. I can make you something which will fit you better than anything you've ever bought off the rack."

"Good luck," I reply. "I don't think there is a truly comfortable suit on the planet — especially not for me."

"Are you issuing me a challenge?" Jordan narrows her gaze and studies me carefully.

"I guess I am. Are you willing to take it on?" I try not to sound too eager. I don't think it would help my cause if she knew I have no other options. The truth is, given her former supervisor's attitude toward other people, I would personally like to see Jordan get all the attention.

Jordan sinks her teeth into her bottom lip. "I don't know your deadline. Honestly, my life is going to be crazy over the next couple of months. Are you sure you're up to this? You'd have to travel to Oregon. There will be multiple fittings."

I just shrug. "I'm flexible. I'm used to traveling. Whatever you need, I've got it."

"What's in this for you?" Jordan's gaze is intense as she studies me. "You have the kind of body designers love. Designers like me make the covers of magazines when people like you wear our clothes. So, why aren't you going with someone with a bigger name?"

I take a seat in her living room. "I met your big-time fashion designer. I didn't like her much. I would rather work with someone who respects other people. So, if I can support the little guy in the fight between good and evil, I'm all about that."

"So, when is this event?" Jordan asks me as she grabs a pad of paper and pen from a little container by her phone. She holds her pen up as if she's poised to write.

"The weekend after the Fourth of July."

Jordan looks up at me in surprise. "Not asking for much, are you? Do you realize the event is only eight weeks away? When you factor in travel time, we wouldn't have much wiggle room. It would take a lot to juggle fittings around both of our schedules — especially since I'm moving. I hate to say this, but I may not be the designer for you. Maybe I've just got too much stuff going on in my life to give you my undivided attention."

"I guess I'll take my chances," I assert, surprising

myself. "I don't want anyone else to work with me. Either you dress me, or I show up at the event wearing boxer shorts."

"Boxer shorts? Why not a Speedo?" she asks with a chuckle. "Then again, those events are so boring, they could use some spice."

"I'd totally stand out on the red carpet, wouldn't I?"

"Trust me, Cristiano, my way is better. Obvious publicity stunts are like a flash in the pan. If we can dress you to match the pictures in my mind, you'll to make a stir without saying a word — as long as you let me do exactly what I want to."

"Am I supposed to be feeling as scared as I am? I'm not used to giving up this much control."

"Well, there's one thing I insist on. I will give you a chance to give all the feedback on the planet, but you have to trust that I know what I'm doing."

"That sounds reasonable to me. I wouldn't want to work with someone who wasn't open to communication going both ways. It's like in a race, your spotter needs to know where you are."

As I watch, Jordan goes over to her coat closet and retrieves a sewing basket. I vaguely remember the contents of all of this from my Home Economics class in junior high school. It's been a while. When Jordan turns around, she has a measuring tape in her hand. It's all I can do not to flinch. My shoulder still hurts from holding my arm up for Mishka.

I try to lift my arm up again and grimace as a white-hot ball of pain hits me.

"Frozen shoulder?" she asks with concern on her face.

I nod as I let my arms fall to my side. "It's not quite frozen yet, but I do have a torn rotator cuff. It hurts like a son of a —" I break off. "That's what I get for messing around with my friends and missing a pro set."

"A what?" Jordan asks as she holds a tape measure up to my arm, writes down the number, and repeats the process as she measures the circumference of my wrist.

"It's a jump in BMX. I was messing around on an old bike with some of my friends. I misjudged the jump."

"Big boys with little toys?"

I smirk. "Pretty much — at least these days. Unfortunately, I keep forgetting I messed up my body to the point where I shouldn't be doing stupid stuff on my bike anymore."

She walks behind me, and I feel her cool hands moving around on my neck as she arranges the measuring tape and writes down some more numbers. "Hmm, no wonder you find off-the-rack clothes so confining," she comments as she places the tape on the top of my shoulders.

"What? Am I freakishly out of proportion?"

She shakes her head. "I've been doing this long enough to know there is no such thing as a typical body type. Everyone is different."

"So, you're telling me you won't have any trouble making clothes to fit me?"

"I can design clothes for your body, I don't know if you'll like them, but I can design them."

"Okay, let's do it How much do these things usually cost?"

Her eyes widen at my question. "You know the old saying? If you have to ask —"

I smile at her snappy retort. "I didn't need a new bike anyway. The moral victory in this will be enough."

"Are you sure? If you'd rather not spend money on an untested designer, I understand."

"No, I'm all the way in. Sometimes, all you need to win the race is a break. Maybe this event will be the break we both could use."

Chapter Three

Jordan

As far as breaks go, this is a pretty good one. I couldn't believe it when Cristiano had a check for a thousand dollars delivered by courier. The sticky note attached said, "Make sure you charge me what is fair. Treat me like any other customer."

Easier said than done; Cristiano is awfully charming. I didn't know what to expect when he landed on my doorstep. After I had taken down all the measurements I needed to create a custom pattern, he took me to Central Park. We got food from Shake Shack and went back to the park for an impromptu picnic. I had so much pent up stress that this was an unexpected, refreshing break from my real life.

Regrettably, it's also where I made a huge fool of myself. Cristiano was chill about it, but I felt stupid. It started out innocently enough. We were doing the whole "get-to-know-you" routine and answering questions about ourselves.

When he talked about his job, I was confused.

Looking at him and seeing his apparent shoulder injury, I figured he might be some sort of stuntman. He's tall, muscular and clearly in shape. When he said he was going to a media event, I assumed it was because he played some role in a movie or television show. I was right — sort of. He is on television, just not the way I imagined. He told me he is in the middle of trying to persuade his executive producer to rename and re-launch a show on ESPN. When I think ESPN, I think football, tennis, or soccer; I don't think X-Games.

I have a hard time wrapping my brain around the concept. To me, the X-Games seem like a bunch of overgrown kids playing in the park. It seems crazy dangerous to be flipping a bike or skateboard around. That's when things went from bad to worse. Apparently, the reason Cristiano is a news commentator who covers the X-Games is because he used to compete in them himself. It's not surprising he found my attitude a little off-putting.

Even though I have a reputation for being blunt — and somewhat witchy — I honestly didn't mean to be snarky. I was just genuinely curious whether people actually follow the X-Games like other sports.

I half expected him to tell me not to bother to make him anything for his event. Trust me to make what would have otherwise been a fun excursion incredibly awkward. For the rest of the afternoon, there was a chill in the air between us. Before I made my inane comments, we'd been laughing and joking about all the places we've been in our lives and exchanging hotel horror stories. Now, I have to figure out a way to bring us back to our original level of cordialness.

Struggling against my nerves, I place my drawing pencil back in the cup and brush the remnants of my eraser off of my pad. I left Mishka's in such a hurry that I left all of my favorite pencils and kneadable eraser in my tote bag in the broom closet. I had hoped to do some drawing on the lunch hour. I never got to take a lunch on the day I left my job, let alone have the opportunity to draw. Now I don't have my art supplies or a job. Things are little screwy when Mishka was the one who was boorish and demeaning, but I'm the one who ended up paying the biggest price. I suppose there are advantages to being the boss.

I can't think about it now, I have to be in presentation mode. Cristiano is on a shoot in Aspen where he's covering the X-Games and we have a video call in a few minutes. After a day of packing and cleaning, I need to make myself somewhat presentable.

After I take a scalding shower, I stand in front of the mirror and look at myself. The blotches caused by my vitiligo are as familiar as a well-worn road map. I wonder what Cristiano would think if he saw me without face and body makeup. I know people with vitiligo who don't bother to cover up. But I've been doing it for so long, it seems like second nature. I started in junior high and just never stopped.

The good news is cover-up makeup has come a long way since then. The bad news is, I'm still not comfortable enough with the way I look to just let it all go. I wish I were the kind of person who could just let the strange looks and criticism roll off my back. Honestly, even as outspoken as I am, I'm still hurt by the stares and remarks. It all bothers me.

Jaxson and I have had many conversations about this. As a doctor, he is well-versed in vitiligo even though it's not his primary specialty. Jaxson is much more laid-back in his life than I am — especially now that he has Gabriel, Donda, and Kennadie. It's amazing how much his teenaged stepson and baby daughter have grounded my brother. He was always wicked smart, but now he is brilliant and happy.

As thrilled as I am for him, I can't seem to make my brother understand we want very different things out of life. For so many reasons I can't even articulate, I'm not sure I see myself in the kind of relationship Jaxson has with Donda. As adorable as Kennadie is, I'm confident I don't want kids and I'm totally okay with not being a parent.

Giving myself a mental shake, I try to turn my thoughts to my call with Cristiano as I quickly put on makeup and a long-sleeved shirt. I haven't done a perfect job of concealing my vitiligo, but in the odd lighting of a video call, I don't think Cristiano will be able to notice much. I pull my hair back into a ponytail and put on my earrings. I tuck my shirt into my jeans and slip on a jacket, so I look professional and put together.

Truth be told, I'm not sure if I'm more nervous about presenting my designs to Cristiano or if I'm just anxious about the prospect of talking to him again since I was such a jerk the last time we spoke. We've been corresponding via email about the design of his suit, and he is exceptionally witty behind the computer screen. Hopefully, the camaraderie we've built online will overshadow my less than graceful performance the other day. I won't get far in the fashion business if I keep insulting my customers — even if it's by accident.

As I wait for Cristiano to call, I arrange the muslin pattern on my dress form. I don't know why I'm even bothering, because I can't adjust the form so it accounts for Cristiano's broad shoulders. I might have to buy a larger one if I continue to work with Cristiano. It's frustrating because I can't tell if the collar will lay correctly without having the bulk of the shoulders in place.

When my computer beeps, I rush over to turn on my camera. When I do, I have to catch my breath. This is a completely different looking Cristiano than I have encountered previously. He is in a shirt, tie, and sports jacket. For a moment, I'm like a guppy caught in a net trying to breathe as I attempt to form words.

"Hi, how are you today?" I know I sound as boring as some of the ladies my mom plays cards with. It's not my fault; the circuits in my brain have been overwhelmed by Cristiano's appearance. I'm having trouble putting together coherent thoughts.

Cristiano shrugs out of his sports coat and sets it beside him on a couch. "Not bad. The weather here has been unpredictable which makes reporting interesting. How about you?" Suddenly, he spots his suit on my dress form. "Are you going to dress me like Colonel Sanders? Why are you making me a white suit? I know his commercials are hot right now, but I don't think I want to go to a swanky event as his double."

"Oh, please tell me there is some event on the planet you'd be willing to go to in a white suit. That would be hysterical."

"Hey, you're supposed to see me as a hot Latino, not some southern gentleman from Kentucky — especially not one who's dead."

I take a moment to appreciate the beauty in front of me. Unfortunately, we are on a video call. My view is limited by his webcam, but he is still a sight to behold. I chuckle softly. "Somehow, I think you probably have enough women in your life who tell you how beautiful you are. Probably happens multiple times a day, right?"

Cristiano has the grace to look embarrassed. "Some days are worse than others … I wouldn't say I go around unnoticed."

"I imagine not. After all, as you said, you're a hot Latino guy."

"I don't have a lot to do with it — it's in the genes. Still, I'll be sure to tell my mom you think her baby is handsome. She'll be happy to hear that."

"Oh, you have one of those too? My mom gushes over my brother and me all the time. You would think we were fashion models or something the way she carries on. She's even worse now that my brother had a baby."

Cristiano's eyebrows climb as he smirks, "Your brother had a baby?"

"No!" I answer with a snort of laughter. "You know what I mean. His wife, Donda, had one. Her name is Kennadie. I can't wait to see her. I've only done FaceTime with them since she was born."

"I bet your family is thrilled about you moving back to Oregon. You'll be there before you know it."

"If you keep reminding me how fast our deadline

is coming up, I'm likely to go into full-on panic mode," I exclaim as I pull up my calendar on my cell phone. "We should probably get in serious planning mode about your outfit for the event. You haven't even told me where this event is."

"If you can believe it," Cristiano says with a soft laugh. "I didn't think to ask Rowden when he told me about it. He just told me to dress up like a decent human being so we could have a shot at wooing the executives at ESPN."

"Oh … kay," I respond as I exhale the breath I've been unconsciously holding. "Nothing like a little pressure on my debut event as a solo designer. You like to make things dangerous, don't you?"

He gives me a smoldering look before he answers, "You have absolutely no idea how dangerous I like things."

I swallow a laugh. "I'm not touching that one with a ten-foot pole."

"Oh come on! You are so much braver on the computer. By the way, I appreciate the fact that you signed me up for a digest of jokes. Unfortunately, most of those aren't jokes I can use on air. They would get me in trouble with the FCC."

"You said you were struggling to come up with material to use on your show, so I thought it would help."

"Back in the day when Rowden and I were just two guys doing a podcast, I would've been all over them. But I have to be a grown up now. I miss the days when I was free to be whoever I wanted to be."

I tighten my lips. "Actually, I haven't been free to be who I am since I turned twelve."

"What do you mean?" Cristiano asks me with open curiosity mixed with what looks like a fair amount of dread.

I laugh at his expression. "Relax, it's not as dramatic as you think. Although, I would love to know what thought just crossed your mind."

"Perhaps I am viewing things through the lens of a little brother — but in my experience, women can be quite dramatic over small stuff."

I start to roll up my sleeve. "We'll be working together, so I might as well tell you. At least you'll be prepared."

"Prepared for what?" He seems perplexed by my odd declaration.

I show him the inside of my wrist which is nearly white. I take a computer wipe out of the package near my monitor and wipe the makeup off my hand as I show him. "I have vitiligo. Don't worry, it's not contagious or anything. It's an autoimmune disorder."

"Isn't that what Michael Jackson had?" he asks.

"Some media reports said he did. I don't know if it was ever verified."

"I was studying you closely the other day. I can't believe I didn't notice. Do you have it all over?"

"That's a pretty personal question, don't you think?" I retort with a crocked smile.

Cristiano blushes again. "Forgive me. I shouldn't have asked. It's not any of my business."

"Don't worry about it. Aside from the question of how contagious I am, it's like the second most common question I get from people. I think it's human nature, we all want to sit around and pick apart each other's lives to make ourselves feel better."

"True enough, but I know how people treat you when you're different. It must be hard to hear everyone's comments."

"I try to tune out the stares and the rude comments. Every once in a while, it still gets to me. Sometimes I wonder if my life would have been easier if I didn't have vitiligo."

"I suppose in some ways it would be easier — how could it not? Yet, think how much you learn about human nature by just being who you are."

"Often, I will learn more than I'd like to." I grimace. "I suppose we better get to talking about business. You never did tell me what your favorite color is."

"I'm a guy. Do most men even have favorite colors? I put on what's clean. Sometimes when I'm really behind on the laundry, it doesn't even have to be clean. It just has to not smell funky."

I cringe as a shudder of disgust travels through my body. "That's so gross. You haven't grown up much from those kids you cover on your show."

"Hey now, before you get too judgmental. Some of those kids are multi-million-dollar celebrities. Like Rowden says, it's not enough just to be an athlete anymore, you have to conquer all the forms of media."

I nod. "That's a lot of pressure. Before you had the

weight of the world on your shoulders, what colors did you like?"

"Honestly, I don't have a favorite. So, I'm leaving all the fashion choices up to you. I'm sure you'll do a better job at figuring it all out than I would."

I stand up and walk over to the dress form as I say, "See, this is part of my problem. What fits on my dress form won't fit you. I'm almost to the point where I need us to get together for a few hours so I can fine tune the pattern before I make it out of expensive cloth."

"So that's what it's for. Hey, I trust your judgment. Make me whatever you think would look good on me."

I grin. "I thought you told me you weren't going to fish for compliments anymore."

Cristiano holds his hands in front of him in a gesture of innocence. "I swear that wasn't what I was doing. I just don't care enough about the colors and all the other garbage to waste your time pretending like I have an actual opinion. I really don't. I just want to look like I fit in with the rest of the crowd there. According to my executive producer, the uppity-ups who make the decisions about our show will be there. They'll be evaluating me and my performance at the event. I need something show-stopping, so people will engage with me and talk."

"Wow! I thought I had a lot of pressure going into this event. I can't imagine being on a job interview which lasted for several hours."

"That's a perfect explanation of what these events are like for me — it's like one big job interview while we all wear penguin suits and sequins. Isn't life strange?"

"Yeah, I agree. If you had told me I'd be designing for an A-List celebrity event, I would have laughed in your face. After all, Mishka treated me as if I was some wayward high school student she had to take under her wing to fix."

"I'm hardly an A-List celebrity. I'm just along for the ride." Cristiano raises a questioning eyebrow at me. "Just out of curiosity, were you a wayward child in high school?"

"Why should I tell you that?" I respond with a gust of laughter. "After all, you could use it against me if you don't like what I design."

Cristiano's brow creases as he lowers his eyebrows in concentration. "I know you don't know me very well, but I'll treat you far better than your former employer. Feel free to share."

"I don't know what you hope to find out," I answer mysteriously.

"Now I really want to know."

"Let's just say … I was an expert at cutting classes and not getting caught."

"Isn't that interesting? I have a similar set of skills, which aren't cool to brag about in normal social settings."

"Someday, we should swap stories. It would be an interesting afternoon," I reply lightly.

"You said I need to try on your fabric thingy, right?"

"You do — the sooner, the better. I've got to get started on making the real thing, or you'll be walking the red carpet naked as a jaybird," I respond with a low laugh.

Cristiano snickers. "Talk about attracting attention

on social media. How about I fly you to Aspen later this week? I'm in post-production on my show, so I can't really get away at the moment. Besides, it would give you a chance to just relax and do nothing in one of the prettiest places on the planet."

"I could pay for my own airline ticket," I protest. "After all, you paid me very well."

"No, the terms of our agreement stipulated I would come to you. However, the events at the X-Games have stacked up because of bad weather, and I can't get away. In order to make this work, I'm going to have to bring you to me. It stands to reason that your trip should be on my dime and not yours. It's my fault I can't come to you."

I chew on the end of my pencil before I roll my shoulder slightly. "I've never actually been to Colorado."

"Great! I'll get my travel agent on it right away. She'll probably be calling you."

"I'll try to pay attention to my phone and not get lost in an artistic fog."

"I've got to go. They're paging me to the set. But, I'm so glad I'm going to get you in my neck of the woods. I think you'll love it here."

"Hey, I won't complain when my job includes a paid vacation," I answer with a wide smile. Sometimes, what seems like bad luck might turn out to be the best luck of all.

Chapter Four

Cristiano

As I glance around my condo, I wonder what I was thinking when I invited Jordan to come visit me. I really do need her to fit me for the suit. Yet, I'm interested in a whole lot more than just her design skills. She fascinates me. She is brash and bold, yet she seems a little shy. I notice this most often when I look at her directly. She seems uncomfortable with any scrutiny. I know from researching Jordan's background online, she is not afraid to put herself on the line — although to be fair, most of the pictures I saw her in seemed to be related to her job at Mishka Unlimited.

There is really no excuse for my condo. I've been here long enough to make changes. I am embarrassed that I haven't even tried. It is a little intimidating to have a designer come to my home. Put politely, my condo is utilitarian. More candidly, it's boring. My sister tried to bring some color into the room. She had a photo of me jumping a little motorcycle over a jump blown up into a stylized painting. Ana Sofía gave it a good college try, but my place needs way more help than my sister could provide.

Maybe imagining what she would do to my place will keep Jordan busy while she's here. Unfortunately, I am slammed with work at the moment and spending more hours than would be considered healthy at the studio. I'm not going have time to play tour guide. There are lots of things to do in Aspen — even during the summer, but I won't have time to show Jordan most of them.

Perhaps I should tell Rowden to take a chill pill. I know trying to get our show noticed by the executives, but all these hours in post-production are driving me crazy. We report on a very fast-moving sport. Conditions are always changing, and as a former athlete, I had to learn to adjust on the fly.

All of these rules, scripts and story ideas are driving me crazy. Professional sports don't operate this way. I don't know if fans need to know all the inner workings of the team. I'm not sure it helps them understand our sport any better. I'm okay with providing my technical expertise to the way riders navigate their way around courses or perform tricks in the air, but this soap opera type environment is not helpful to portraying people in our sport as serious athletes. These rivalries which are pumped up by the director and Rowden drive me insane.

When I was active in the X-Games, there were people we didn't necessarily get along with as well as other people, but we kept those rivalries to ourselves — to do anything else is considered unprofessional. I am afraid the media spotlight and pressure will change the nature of our sport.

As soon as we hit a lull in our coverage, we need to address all of this. Honestly, I'm not sure how much weight I have with him. I suppose he could just as easily replace me as the on-air talent. There are a lot of ex-bikers out there. There may be someone else who wants to try their hand at analyzing races. So, I have to bite my tongue.

My phone buzzes with a text message from Jordan; her plane is about to land. I glance up at the clock in surprise. I'm not exactly sure how this day got away from me, but here I am. I don't feel prepared for this visit at all. My nerves won't solve anything. Jordan will be here one way or another. I guess I'll have to wing it. It wouldn't be the first time I've pulled a strategy out of thin air.

⬤ ● ⬤

"Are you sure you don't want me to get a rental car?" Jordan asks as we walk out to my rig. "I would hate to be a bother."

"Don't be silly. You're no bother. Unfortunately, I have some less than optimal news. I'll be working pretty much nonstop during the next two days because we're doing some final production work on the series. So, I won't be able to escort you around town. I can ride my bike to work and you can have my car. That's not a problem. There are all sorts of cool restaurants, spas and art galleries around. Knock yourself out while I'm at work. Don't think you need to stick around my condo."

"You live in a condo? For some reason, I had you pegged as an old house kind of guy — you know …

plantation style."

"I would dig an antebellum mansion with big old columns and scrollwork. I'd love to be able to plan my programs while I swing on the front porch. Unfortunately, there aren't many homes like that around Aspen. Besides, I travel most of the year. Having a big place is not very practical for me. Basically, my condo is a place where I fall down and collapse when I'm too tired to do anything else."

Jordan looks thoughtful. "I don't know if I can imagine that. To me, home is like my safety zone. It's where I feel the most relaxed and creative — my getaway from the rest of the world."

I open the car door for her and take her purse and set it on the pile of luggage at my feet. "I'll just stick this in the back for you unless you need it. Would you like to go grab a bite to eat?"

"I don't think I'll need any of it for a while." Jordan tries to draw her hair up into a ponytail and wind a hair tie around it. She blows out an exasperated breath and rolls her eyes. "Are you sure you want to be seen with me? I am a mess right now because of the bizarre air on the plane. It makes my hair do all sorts of crazy things it wasn't doing this morning after my shower."

Her comments take me by surprise because Jordan looks beautiful. She is wearing blue jeans, a tank top and off-the-shoulder T-shirt. Jordan looks relaxed and comfortable. Her hair is wild and free which is my favorite way to see it. I know from dealing with my sister most women don't like their curly hair. But, Jordan's hair just begs for my fingers to be in it.

When I pause too long Jordan looks at me expectantly, so I shake my head at her to show her what a mess my hair is. "You're in good company. I need a haircut so bad I can almost taste it. I haven't had time to do it. Even the stage manager has started calling me 'mountain man'."

"I could take care of it for you if you want me to. I mean, I'm not a professional stylist or anything, but I used to take care of kids a lot. Many times, their parents didn't want to spend money to go to high-priced salons, so I learned to cut their hair on my own."

Skeptical, I run my hands through my hair and respond, "This is pretty complicated. There are layers and highlights going on. Are you sure you can handle it?"

"Oh, Lawdy! Why didn't you tell me you were a problem child?" she teases. "Then again, I guess I could've taken one look at you and figured it out for myself. Boys as pretty as you are usually high maintenance."

I cringe at her words. "I don't suppose there's anything I can do to convince you I'm not one of those guys. Yeah, I've got an expensive haircut and highlights in my hair, but it wasn't my idea. I'd rather be covered in mud and going around a racetrack or flying in the air, wearing a beanie. This suave, sophisticated newscaster personality isn't exactly who I am. I'm one of those guys who lets loose with cuss words when I watch soccer and basketball. I like to eat churros, Doritos, and Pepsi while I stand in front of my pantry or refrigerator in my underwear. Don't let appearances fool you."

Jordan studies me with an intense expression. "If

you are in the habit of cussing, how do you stop yourself from doing it on air when you are watching a race? I'm afraid if someone let me out in front of the cameras, I would give everyone around me a heart attack."

I smile at Jordan's confession. "It sounds like we are a lot alike. Rowden and Jubilee have an anxiety attack every time I go on the air. It's hard to stay neutral. Personally, I have my favorites, but I'm not supposed to let anyone know. Opinions are not popular in my line of work."

Jordan nods. "I get that. It's something I struggle with. Sometimes, I can't keep my opinions to myself. Although after I hurt my sister-in-law so deeply she almost broke up with my brother, I've been a little more circumspect about sharing my opinions."

"No joke? You almost broke up your brother's marriage?"

"Yeah, it was pretty close. I tried to convince him Donda wasn't the woman of his dreams. Basically, I had no idea what I was talking about. I judged her on her outside appearance and her circumstances. I had no concept of the pain and suffering she'd been through in her life."

"I take it you have a different opinion of her now?"

"It's safe to say that. Actually, once I got over my hurt feelings over the fact my brother was moving on with his life after the death of his daughter, Jasmine, I discovered Donda and her son Gabriel are the pieces of the puzzle my brother needed to make his life complete. They are a remarkable family."

"Didn't you tell me you have another niece?" I ask

trying to follow the conversation.

"Yeah, I have a niece named Kennadie now. At one point, I had a niece named Jasmine too. Her mother was so high on drugs, and she didn't notice she left my niece in a hot car while she partied."

"Donda's drug use?" I ask incredulously. "I thought you told me the last time we were together your brother is some fancy orthopedic doctor. I would think something like drug abuse might be detrimental to his career."

"No, he met Donda much later. Donda has her own son, Gabriel. Jasmine died so long ago that if she had lived, she would be in college now."

"Oh wow! Your brother started over again?"

Jordan laughs out loud as she loosens her seatbelt a bit so she can move more easily in the car. She turns toward me and says, "Yes, in a way. Isn't it wild? I was mad in the beginning too. I was sure Jaxson was trying to replace Jasmine. I finally figured out they weren't really planning anything. I know if anything like that happened to me, I would be completely lost."

"I think you've done a remarkable job dealing with all the changes in your life. You don't seem lost to me. You're here with me — designing clothes. That's progress, right?"

Jordan smiles at me as she scolds, "Oh, stop trying to get me to drop hints about your suit. You told me you trusted me to handle whatever was thrown at me."

I scrunch up my face in displeasure. "I'm busted. You know me, I'm a racer. Waiting around for an outcome is not my favorite thing to do."

Jordan laughs at my expression. "Have patience. I need to wait a bit until I'm sure I've got everything lined up. I'll do my full reveal soon, I promise."

"You know, we never did talk about what would happen if the suit wasn't finished or I absolutely hate it … or if you despise it," I comment.

Jordan grimaces. "It's like you're inside my head. Chances are I'll absolutely hate it before you even have an opportunity to see it. That's usually how my process works. I start out with a very good idea and then as I design the outfit piece by piece and then tear it apart for a pattern, I begin to see all the things I could do better or differently. It seems I'm never actually truly happy with the work I do."

I chuckle softly as I reply, "I know what you mean. I spend so much time in post-production trying to fix what I've already done. It's absolutely crazy. I don't like my voice on tape. To me, it always seems like I'm not speaking clearly enough or my accent is coming across too strong."

"I can't imagine having a chance to redo your conversations in real time. If it were me, I would say something completely different each and every time, and they would never be able to splice it together into a coherent thought."

"You'd be amazed how often it happens — even when I'm repeating stuff from a script. I often have to do clean-up work simply because I didn't remember what I was supposed to say the first time."

"I bet it's worse than having a college professor

hand back your work and tell you to redo it according to their style. I thought it was okay to be bold and fearless and beauty was subjective. I learned otherwise when I went to school. I got so sick of the criticism, I changed my major to journalism. It seemed like a safe backup plan, and I figured if nothing else, it might give me access to clients I might not otherwise have."

"Way to think ahead," I compliment with a grin. "Your approach to career planning is better than mine. I basically have spent a lifetime bouncing between one race and another and one career move after another."

"Are you telling me your whole entire existence is a series of happy accidents, one after the other?" Jordan asks with her eyes wide.

I nod "I suppose you could chalk my whole career up to a series of accidents. However, not all of them were happy or healthy. Sometimes, my biggest successes have been built on even bigger failures."

"What do you mean?" Jordan studies me.

"Well, the X-Games are a young person's game. Even before I did the idiotic thing at the race track with my friends, my body was falling apart piece by piece. I knew I would have to do something to survive after my body quit. I just didn't expect it to quit before the age of forty."

Jordan looks away and starts to watch out the side window. I'm not sure how I've offended her, but she is rigid, and the atmosphere is oddly tense as she actively pretends I'm not in the small car with her.

I decide to stay quiet for a while. I don't even know what to say to her. We don't have the kind of relationship where I feel comfortable pressing Jordan to talk about whatever is bothering her. After all, I'm just a guy getting a suit. I don't have the right to ask about personal information in her life unless she shares it. I lean forward to tune the radio to a pop station. "We have a way to go before we get to my condo and it looks like traffic is pretty messed up. Why don't you go ahead and get some rest until we get to my place?"

"I'm sorry to be such a witch. My flight took off ridiculously early this morning, and I am more than cranky."

"Why don't you rest? You'll have plenty of time to go exploring later."

"I think I'll do that," she says as she yawns. "I tend to get carsick anyway. It's not a pretty sight."

I reach over to turn down the radio and adjust the heat. "I bet not. I'll wake you if I run across anything which merits notice."

Jordan shrugs as she sheds her jacket and props it against the window as she relaxes.

"I'm sorry I'm such boring company," she mumbles. "I'm just exhausted."

"Whatever we have to talk about, can wait until after you have a good rest and a good meal," I respond as I lower the volume on the radio.

"Okay," she says, fighting a yawn.

"You can relax. I've got the driving covered. I'll wake you up when we get home."

The word home is not usually one I wax poetic about. However, there is something about this situation which has me looking at all sorts of different areas in my life in a new light.

CHAPTER FIVE

JORDAN

I DON'T KNOW WHAT I expected from Cristiano's place, but this isn't it. For a guy who seems larger-than-life and full of spark and energy, this place feels like a misfire. The nicest thing I can say about it is the gray is likely to hide a lot of dirt. My brain and my fingers are itching to get started on making everything fit. I have to remind myself I'm not here to work on his home. I have other things to accomplish.

Cristiano massages his shoulder as he walks up beside me. "You don't have to say anything. Your face says it all. Don't worry. I pretty much feel the same way about this place. I got it for dirt cheap because the former tenants needed to move overseas for their new teaching jobs. It was basically a cement-colored box when I moved in. I just haven't had much of a chance to do anything with it. To be honest, I really haven't had any motivation to make this place anything more than a temporary home."

"What's wrong? Don't you like Aspen?" I ask.

"Everything I've heard about it makes it seem like it's a phenomenal place to live."

"It's not that. The city itself is beautiful enough. The food here is delicious, and the art scene is kind of cool — if that's what you're into."

"Not surprisingly, I am into the art scene." I raise an eyebrow.

"I expected you would be. I suppose I could probably be into it too — or any number of other things … except most of those things require someone to share the experience with. I am pretty isolated here. My family lives a long way from here."

I'm not able to cover my skepticism as I glance over at Cristiano. "Are you telling me someone who looks like you has a difficult time finding suitable company?"

He rubs the back of his neck. "As odd as it sounds … yes."

"Okay, this is going to make me sound insecure and weird — but for someone like me who has to hide who I am to prevent other people from being repulsed, I have a hard time believing someone who looks like you has any problems."

"If all I wanted was to pick some girl up, I'd have no difficulty. I decided I deserve more. I want someone who has some brains between their ears and some compassion in their heart. Forget online dating. It's a wasteland out there. I don't know if it's the fact that I'm on television now, or that people can look me up on the Internet and realize I spent some time at the top of the winners' podium; but these days, most women seem to think of me as one big fat wallet," Cristiano explains.

"Well, that's just rude."

"I don't want a relationship based on money. I want someone who understands who I really am as a person — Geez, I sound like a motivational poster."

The look on Cristiano's face is so forlorn I feel bad for cracking the joke. "If that's how you really feel, I wouldn't apologize for it. I share your pain with the online dating thing, I stopped going out to coffee with people. The last three guys I dated felt if they treated me to a latte with whipped cream, it meant I had to treat them to a whole bevy of sexual services. That's not what I'm about. I mean, I have no objection to great lovemaking, but that's not why I go to coffee with a stranger."

His eyes widen. "Okay, that's wrong and creepy. Where do they find these people?"

"I guess the dating companies have studied us all very carefully like lab rats. They know we have a need to be with someone. It's like an instinctual compulsion."

Cristiano gives me a tight smile. "I think you're right. For some reason, even though my life is pretty happy right now, I feel like I'm missing something. When I score a great interview or am able to call a race cleanly with no mistakes, I want to come home and celebrate with someone."

"It's hard to be single. Every event is geared toward couples, and even if your friends are understanding, they always flinch a bit when you tell them you're not bringing anyone. Sometimes I wonder if I should just buy a novelty blow-up doll and dress him as some stud-like lumberjack. I think it would be funny to cart him around to different social events."

Cristiano grins. "I don't know how amused people would be, but you would make your point. I hate to admit this, but some of the women I've dated recently have been such airheads that there's very little difference between them and a blow-up doll."

My eyes widen. "Wow! That's harsh. Way to be a jerk!"

"I swear, I'm not being a jerk. I'm not that kind of guy. I'm just saying I don't know what happens to people when they start dating. I once took a woman out for lunch who spent fifty-seven minutes talking about the Barbie collection she started when she was three years old. I guess I expected more from the conversation because she was a very successful PR rep."

I laugh out loud. "I suppose fifty-seven minutes is better than an hour."

"Yeah ... everyone's a comedian until you have to sit and listen to someone describe little, bitty Barbie outfits in excruciating detail. She knew where every stitch and snap and button were on each outfit. It was a little creepy."

"That's almost as weird as the guy I went out with who knew every single character from every Shirley Williams show ever made — even the ones who weren't from blockbuster musicals."

Cristiano chuckles. "It's a shame we can't play matchmaker for the two of our failed dates. They sound like they might actually get along."

I play his scenario and in my mind for a bit before I say, "Weirdly, I think you're probably right. Wouldn't it be funny if there was like a Goodwill selection for dates which didn't work out? You could go in and exchange your date for another one who is a better match."

"That would be very dangerous for me — can you imagine if all the women I'd ever dated got together in one room to talk?"

"Trust me — with my tendency to blurt out inappropriate things, I wouldn't fare any better. The guys wouldn't be bored when they compared stories that's for sure."

"How did we get started talking about dating?" Cristiano asks as he scratches his neck. "I was just telling you about my ugly condo. We've gone pretty far off course."

"Don't worry. My brain is working overtime to figure out how to make this place match your personality. About the only thing I like is the beautiful painting on your wall."

"Now whose turn is it to be harsh?" Cristiano asks with a laugh. "Seriously, my sister had it made for me. It's also my favorite thing in the apartment."

I look down at my toes and blush. "Yeah, I tried to warn you about my tendency to blurt out rude things. I didn't mean it as a criticism, just as an observation."

"I was just teasing, Jordan. My apartment needs tons of help. If you can help me with that, I would really appreciate it."

"You're not joking?" I ask incredulously. "The one piece of artwork is the only thing in your whole apartment you like? No wonder you don't feel at home here. If you hate the things that surround you, it's never going to feel right."

"Well, I like the painting, and I like my bed. I splurged on a great one. If I had my way, I would crawl into it and sleep for about a month. I've been on the road so much, the airport personnel are going to start greeting me by my first name like they do on TV when people go to their favorite diner or bar."

"You really travel that much?" My stomach does a little somersault when I think about all the stress that would cause for me. "If I'm not working, I'm at home. At this point, a good TV dinner and my favorite Netflix movie on television are about as adventurous as I get."

Cristiano shakes his head as he responds, "Are you kidding me? You flew to Aspen to fit my suit. You're telling me you're not adventurous?"

"I wasn't ... not until I met you."

"I didn't know the meaning of word 'couture' until I met you. I guess we've both changed a little." Cristiano glances around. "Are you good with pizza for tonight? I don't know about you. I'm beat."

"Let's just say, my early flight spent a lot of time on the runway. I can never sleep on a plane."

"I'll take that as a yes. What kind of pizza would you like?" Cristiano takes a refrigerator magnet off his fridge and shows it to me.

"I'm not picky. Long as it's got a thin crust and some chicken on it."

Cristiano takes out his phone and starts to dial.

"Don't you need a menu to order from?" I ask.

"Don't worry about it, I order from this place so

often they should probably name their entire line of pizzas after me."

"How long does it take this place to make pizza? I really need a shower. Did I mention someone's service dog threw up on me?"

"Knock yourself out. There are some clean towels in the spare bathroom."

"You know what? I can wait until I get to my hotel. I don't feel up to digging through all my stuff."

Cristiano looks chagrined. "Uh … I didn't book you a hotel."

"You didn't book me a hotel?" my eyes widen, and I swallow hard. A thousand thoughts tumble around in my brain as I think about all the safety protocols I've broken around Cristiano. My gut tells me it'll be totally fine — but then again, my gut has been a little screwy these days. It's not like I have a lot of choice. Even though Cristiano is paying me well, my bank balance wouldn't cover the coast of lodging in Aspen. Talk about your awkward situations.

I clear my throat. "Umm … why?"

Cristiano shrugs. "Figured you could stay here. It's not as if I don't have enough room. Heck, you could throw a party here, and it probably wouldn't bother me."

I breathe a sigh of relief at his answer. At least he doesn't seem to expect me to sleep in his bed. Gamely, I put on a happy face as I admit, "I haven't stayed with a guy I just met since college. This could be interesting. I wasn't planning any parties, but a shower sure would be heaven."

"I swear I'm an awesome roommate. I won't steal your clothes or borrow your makeup. They said the pizza will be here in about forty-five minutes. Just watch the shower head. If it gets stuck in position five, the water comes out like bullets."

"Thanks, although I may need that setting to keep me awake the way I'm feeling."

"If you need anything fancier than a bar of white soap, check under the sink. Ana keeps her bubbles and stuff there."

"Ana?" I ask, not recognizing the name.

Cristiano smiles at me. "My sister, Ana Sofía — she house-sits for me sometimes. She enjoys all that foofy girl stuff."

I smile gratefully at him. A guy who keeps frilly stuff around for his sister can't be so bad. "That sounds heavenly. It's been a long time since I have had a chance to pamper myself."

"Pamper away. I'll be downstairs trying to contain my exploding inbox if you need anything."

When I walk past Cristiano, I reach out to touch his long hair behind his ear and run the back of my fingers down his cheek. "You might just be too sweet for your own good."

"Um … okay. I'll let you know when the pizza gets here. Want anything special to drink? I could rustle up some decent wine if you'd like."

"Something feels off about this. You shouldn't have to be working so hard to keep me entertained. I am supposed to be working for you, and now you're sending me for a luxury bath, ordering pizza and offering wine?"

Cristiano smiles. "Don't worry — tomorrow will be soon enough for me to start taking advantage of your skills."

⸺●⸺

"Bend your elbow, please," I mumble around the pins I'm holding in my mouth. I forgot to bring my wrist pincushion, so this is a little awkward. If I'm going to take my show on the road, I need to plan better. I always forget how many tools I use in my trade — at least, I do until I need to use them.

I pull my dressmakers chalk out of my pocket and mark the correct hemline on his sleeve.

"I know this is just a rough pattern, but I am amazed. I can actually bend my arm without the jacket being tight," Cristiano comments as he flexes his arm again.

"Welcome to the marvelous world of custom-made clothes. A place where things actually fit your body, instead of some anonymous nonexistent body type dreamed up by some marketing person to represent the perfect body. Most of us do not have figures like that."

"You're telling me — I haven't been able to comfortably fit into clothes since I was a teenager. It always seems like something is too tight or too short."

I can't help but smile a self-satisfied smile as I watch him move around in my simple muslin pattern. In my mind, it's a gorgeous charcoal summer-weight wool paired with a green and blue hued silk tie — something to subtly reinforce his company's logo.

"If you think that's great, why don't you bend down and try to tie your shoes?"

"Would if I could." When I frown, Cristiano shows me his feet with oversized Bigfoot slippers. "Should I wear these with the suit?"

"Personally, as your stylist, I would recommend something a little more formal. Although, I do think your slippers are radically cool."

"I hate having to dress up to go on air. I'd much rather be wearing sweats and my slippers."

"Well, I have good news for you. Once we develop these patterns for you, they can be adapted a bunch of ways. So, the days of you having to squeeze into somebody else's definition of normal are over."

"You mean I can call you and say, 'Hey, I need a navy-blue suit for a meeting,' and you can do that? No more trips to the mall?"

I can't help but smile at his disbelief. "That's the idea."

"I feel classed-up now." Cristiano shoots me a charming grin as he says, "You might have spoiled me for life. I might have to keep you around."

As hard as I try to come up with a downside to his proposition, nothing is coming to mind.

Chapter Six

Cristiano

Jordan grabs me by the arm as she drags me down the aisle of the home decorating store. "Why do you look petrified? I thought you were some big shot Olympic athlete. Shouldn't you be a little braver?" Jordan laughs at the petrified expression on my face. It is obvious Jordan is comfortable in this space. I've never seen her be so carefree.

"Unfortunately, I didn't get my shot at being an Olympian. They didn't add motocross to the Olympics until after I retired."

Jordan stops in the middle of the aisle and turns to me. "I still can't get over the fact that you are already retired. It's just bizarre."

"I tell myself the same thing nearly every day when I look in the mirror. My body just quit before I wanted it to."

"It's not exactly the same, but I felt something like that about my vitiligo. When I was a kid, it started out as a spot under my arm and on the side of my breast. It looked almost as if I had spilled bleach on myself. For a long time, I hid it from everyone, even my family. I was scared I was dying of some sort of skin cancer. I mean, I had heard of vitiligo because of my mother's obsession with Michael Jackson. Even so, I never associated it with an ordinary person. I was so scared, I could barely breathe. I tried to take as few baths as possible and ultimately gave up swimming. I got in trouble in PE class because I didn't want to change my clothes in front of others. Much to my horror, one spot became many and I wasn't able to hide it."

Scrutinizing her carefully, I remark, "If you hadn't told me you had vitiligo, I would never have guessed. Don't you get makeup on your clothes?"

"Sometimes, if it's scorching outside and I'm sweating, it will come off more easily than other times. For the most part, the brand I use is pretty stable on my skin. I try to make sure I blend it in really carefully; and I tend to wear brown, yellow, and orange clothes, so it doesn't show if it does come off."

"You know, you don't have to wear all of that stuff around me. Vitiligo isn't contagious. I'm not going to judge you because you have it."

She turns around and faces me as she starts to walk backward down the aisle. "I understand you are compassionate and accepting. However, the rest of the world doesn't necessarily think the same way. I'd rather not deal with the stares and other strange behavior. I've gotten so used to covering it all up, it would feel odd for me not to."

"Whatever makes you comfortable. Just know I'm

okay either way. I think you are beautiful."

"When you say things like that, it's enough to make even me swoon," she answers as she bats her eyelashes playfully. "Seriously, I'll keep it in mind. Sometimes, the whole makeup routine gets itchy and intrusive, and someday I might just take it all off."

"I understand. I'm pretty compulsive about using sunscreen because we do so many outside shoots, but I still hate the way sunscreen feels on my skin. Sometimes, I'd like to skip it."

Jordan looks horrified. "Oh please don't. My mom had a cancer scare a few years ago, and it was enough to nearly tear our family apart. If you can save yourself the trouble, it's worth it."

"Wow, you have had your share of problems, haven't you?"

"Recently, yes. I hope the move to Oregon will give me a fresh start and I can repair the damage I've done to my family. I feel awful about the way I treated them all. I don't know what came over me, but there are so many things I would change about the way I dealt with everyone. I hope they give me a chance to start over."

I grasp her hand and hold it in mine. "I can't imagine they wouldn't. Families are resilient. If you can tell them exactly what you just said to me, I think it would probably go a long way to repair your relationship. At least, it does with me."

Jordan squeezes my hand. "I don't know why some woman somewhere hasn't snapped you up. You are probably one of the nicest guys I've ever met."

I blush. "Don't be fooled. Not all of me is nice. I am fiercely competitive and I can be hyper-focused on things which take away time from a healthy relationship. It's no picnic being with me. I am like an overgrown teenager in a grown-up's body. Most women find me terribly annoying."

"I can see where they might, but if they look deep enough, they'll find you have a wonderful, empathetic spirit."

"I know you'll accuse me of fishing for compliments, but I'm not. I struggle with the way people treat me based on my looks. It's pure genetics — I have nothing to do with it. However, when you combine my appearance with the fact that I was, for a while, a professional athlete, it's a double-edged sword. People don't look behind my appearance to find out who I really am. I suppose it's probably at the real root of why I'm single."

The corner of Jordan's mouth lifts up in a crooked grin as she silently challenges me. I put my hands in front of me in a gesture of protest as I say, "What's that look for? I want someone to be attracted to the real me and not just what I look like. After all, this could all be very temporary. People are disfigured in accidents and by disease all the time. So, if I'm going to settle down and be with someone, I want them to be in love with all of me and not because I make good arm candy."

Jordan laughs lightly. "I'm sorry to break it to you Cristiano, but people will always focus on the way you look because you are an exceptionally handsome man. It's the thing that will get the most notice. You just have to persuade someone to stick around long enough to see the real you."

I sigh. "Maybe that's my problem. Perhaps I don't stick around in one spot long enough to attract the right kind of woman."

Jordan smiles at me. "If the woman of your dreams comes back to your condo, I can understand why she might not want to stay. Your condo doesn't say anything good about you. In fact, it sort of screams serial killer."

"Really? How do you figure?" I ask her with open skepticism.

"Don't you watch any horror movies? The serial killer always lives in an apartment with absolutely no personalization. They all look like strange hotel rooms in the movies — kinda like your condo," she teases.

"Okay," I answer with a laugh. "I get the point. So, that's why I'm here on a Saturday against my will. I suppose you're doing it for my own well-being —"

"You bet. Do you think I'm here for my own health and gratification? I would just as soon have stayed in bed."

"Actually, I think you're here because you want to torture me with shopping in a place which vaguely smells like perfume. If I ever become filthy rich, I would have someone else do all my shopping for me."

"These days with everything in my life up in the air, I think about winning the lottery a lot. It would be nice not to have to work quite so hard for our dreams."

"Something tells me even if I won the lottery, I'd still be working hard at something. I'm just one of those people who has to succeed and compete. I don't think I would make a very successful millionaire beach bum — well, with the exception of having someone else do all my shopping … and maybe cooking."

"At the moment I'm so tired, I'll stipulate I would make a spectacular millionaire beach bum. I wouldn't even need any exceptions."

I shake my head. "You say that now, but you are a lot like me. You are driven, focused and just as competitive as I am."

Jordan laughs. "You're probably right. I think it's the little sister syndrome. I always wanted to do everything Jaxson did — except better."

"Maybe that's what happened with me. I am the quintessential little brother. I was always in my sister's business and trying to be as good at everything as she was. In fact, I think that's why my dad introduced me to BMX bikes and motocross. My parents were desperate to give my sister some breathing room. I idolized her so much I followed her around everywhere. She probably thought it was the most annoying thing on the planet. However, I didn't even care. I wanted to learn as much from her as I possibly could."

"So, what does your big sister do now?" Jordan asks as she picks up a couple of throw pillows and compares them.

"Would you believe she is a pit boss at one of the Indian casinos? Ana Sofía has been there six years now."

"I bet it makes for some interesting people watching. People come to casinos for very different reasons."

"I don't know. We don't talk about it much because my sister keeps odd hours, and so do I. Being away from New Mexico is hard."

"It sounds like you're due for a visit home. You seem exceptionally homesick."

"As much as I travel, you would think I would visit home more often. I do miss my family. I have a few fences to mend with Ana Sofía. I have been putting it off for too long." I shake my head as if to clear my thoughts as I paste a smile on. "Let's go find some stuff to match my painting. If my place is as bad as you say it is, no wonder my family doesn't come to visit very often."

Jordan looks down at the floor and then away. "Maybe I'm too sensitive to all of this as a designer, but your condo is pretty bad."

"I totally agree with you. It's downright depressing. Let's change that," I reply, as I kick the squeaky tire of our cart.

"What things do you want to change? You are the one who has to live there."

"I'm really not home much. When I am, I like to be comfortable. I don't feel comfortable in a fussy environment."

"I agree with you. I don't think it matches your personality very well."

"This I have to hear — what do you believe matches my personality? Is this like one of those tests you take on the Internet? 'Does your house match who you are?'" I tease.

"Go ahead, make fun of it — but I bet after we

make all these changes, you will feel more comfortable in your own house. There is something to be said about making your surroundings match your approach to life. You might even begin to have more company once your house reflects who you are."

"I don't know about that. I am really not all that social."

"Okay, I guess we won't do a huge dining table which seats sixteen or anything —"

"Do they make dining room tables that huge? A table like that would thrill my mother. She would love to come here at Christmas time and have a huge family gathering."

"Is it something you want? You have tons of space. It's totally doable."

"I don't know. Let me think about it. I've never thought of my condo as anything but a place to crash when I was too tired to do anything else."

"Is there anything specific you want us to look at? Do you like your bedding to be fluffy or streamlined and sleek?"

"It gets cold here in the winter, I would like a down comforter."

"Anything else?" Jordan asks as she writes notes on her phone.

I sigh impatiently. "I don't know. I guess I never thought about it. The picture Ana Sofía gave me makes me happy. I had some great times racing."

"Okay, so we'll make it the focal point of your living room and build from there. We don't have to make huge changes, I think you just need some texture and color in your house to make it feel less industrial."

"I just thought of something. It frustrates me that when it's cold outside, I don't have a good way to sit in front of the fireplace. The owners who had the place before me paid big bucks to have a functional fireplace. I always feel guilty when I don't take advantage of it."

"That's understandable. The marble used to make the fireplace is beautiful. So, why don't we add a seating area?"

"Okay, I'm getting the hang of this. Let the adventure begin. You'll tell me if I go radically wrong, won't you?"

"I have a hard time keeping my opinions to myself. Unfortunately for you, I probably won't make an exception for you."

"Bring it on. I'm in hunter mode. I am ready to make my place presentable."

Jordan smirks at me. "You might want to be careful what you wish for, I'm pretty good at spending other people's money." With that, she tosses a couple of brightly colored throw pillows in the basket.

"I have a feeling that I'm going to be in the race of my life today. I'm looking forward to the challenge."

<hr>

I reach out and massage Jordan's shoulders when I notice she is rolling her neck and trying to stretch out her back. "If you would've told me fixing up my cement box would be such a strenuous workout, we would've done some warm-up exercises. I can't believe we have four carts worth of stuff."

"This is only part of it. They have to get more from the stockroom." Jordan leans into my touch. "Mmm … I think I'll let you follow me everywhere I go from now on. This feels amazing," she purrs.

When the line moves forward, I have to pull away and move our carts. A cheerful middle-aged woman with bright red hair examines the things in our carts. "Redoing the kid's room? I bet you guys have some adorable little rugrats."

Out of the corner of my eye, I see Jordan's lips thin, and her face fill with tension. "We don't have kids. I'm just his designer," Jordan protests.

The woman clicks her tongue at Jordan. "That's a darn shame. There are just some people who should make babies together, and I have a hunch the two of you would make great parents."

As a professional athlete, I get occasional comments about superior DNA and making babies to preserve my legacy. Usually, I laugh them off. Yet, Jordan does not seem to be amused, so I dig out my wallet and place my credit card on the check stand. "I don't think I will be making any random children with my designer anytime soon, thank you," I declare calmly as I challenge the cashier's assumptions with my gaze. "I'd like twenty dollars cash back, please."

Turning to Jordan, I ask, "Do you think we'll get this all in the rig?"

"We probably could, if we're creative with packing. I figured, with your shoulder injury, you'd rather pay for delivery."

"See? That's why I hang out with you. You do things the smart way."

Jordan gives the woman the side-eye as she responds, "Thanks. I'd like to think I am capable of making solid decisions occasionally."

As we wait for the paperwork to get squared away, Jordan and I buy coffee from a little in-store kiosk. After I take a sip of my latte, I comment, "That was a bit awkward. Talk about a total lack of boundaries."

Jordan sighs. "You have no idea what it's like. Everyone has expectations — even people I've never met. Sometimes it gets exhausting. It's not possible for me to be everything everyone wants me to be."

I reach across the table and grab Jordan's hand. "I don't know. You've been pretty much everything I need you to be even when I didn't know what that is."

"That may actually be the nicest thing anyone has said to me in a while. Thank you," Jordan answers with a shaky smile.

⬤

I can't believe the week with Jordan has passed by so quickly. It makes me a little sad to see her sorting her boarding pass out from the rest of her paperwork. I don't even know if I can formulate coherent things to say to her right now. It's not like we did anything spectacular or unique while she was here. Her presence makes me more optimistic about life. I know it sounds strange — I am around people every day. Some of them are good friends from the racing world, yet Jordan's existence in my life seems to be a grounding force. Even though we just met, I feel like I can simply be Cristiano Jorge Romero around her without feeling like I have to live up to some storied past or uncertain future. Honestly, I'd be happy if she stayed here with me. I know staying put doesn't fit with her plans.

"You're quiet today." Jordan hitches her backpack up on her shoulder. "Are you hurting?"

"Yes and no," I answer candidly. "My shoulder is feeling okay today, but I'm still feeling off."

"What do you mean?" Jordan studies me.

I escort her over to a row of seats in the terminal which are off the beaten path. After we sit down, I reply, "Bear with me, this is going to take a bit of explanation —"

"Do I want to hear this?"

"I hope so. When I went into Mishka's shop, I expected to find some pretentious clothes I probably wouldn't want to wear for more than a couple of hours. I didn't anticipate I'd find a friend. It's been years since I have made any true buddies. After I was injured, I learned the hard way that the people who were there for me were few and far between. The fact that you trusted me enough to come and stay with me while you design my suit, means a lot to me — in ways I can't even explain."

"Cristiano, it was no big deal. I understand why you couldn't come to me. Maybe the next time you can," Jordan responds.

"You know this thing between us goes deeper than just travel arrangements, right? I'm profoundly sad you're going to be going back home to New York."

"You have no idea what your words mean to me. The fact that you accepted me even though I am full of flaws means a whole lot to me too."

"So, what are we going to do about our geography?"

"On the positive side, Oregon is closer to Aspen than New York —"

I reach out and pull her into a loose embrace. "Right … we can handle this. I'm in the air most the time anyway, I'll simply arrange my travel schedule, so I have more layovers in Portland."

"I like the sound of that. I'm glad you don't plan to disappear from my life after I finish designing your suit. I would miss you too much." Jordan wipes away tears.

Chapter Seven

Jordan

"I LOVE YOUR NEW place," I comment to my sister-in-law, Donda. "You guys weren't kidding when you said you had space for me. I didn't expect to have half of the whole upstairs."

"I'm sorry it's not completely finished yet. I had plans to redesign the entire space, so it's more historically accurate — but to be honest having a baby at my age is more than a little exhausting. Now that Kennadie can get around on her own, I feel like I'm chasing her all day, every day. Even though I work from home, it is incredibly difficult for me to get anything done."

"I bet having Brando around doesn't help matters." I scoop Gabriel's French bulldog puppy up off the floor and cuddle him to my chest. "Hopefully, I'll be able to take some pressure off — at least until I find myself another career. Unfortunately, I haven't figured out how to find a job when I unceremoniously quit my last one. I'm still not sure if Mishka has the clout to blacklist me. I'm a little afraid to apply for work in fashion."

"It is hard. Gabriel's father was a drug addict. He kept moving us around to evade law enforcement. I was forever starting new jobs only to have to quit later. My own issues didn't help matters — so, I can relate. Let me know if I can do anything. I'd appreciate your help if you got some time to consult on a couple of jobs. I've got one client who isn't sharing my vision for her space. Maybe a set of fresh eyes would help us get past our impasse."

"Are you sure? You design living spaces for other people — that can be exacting. Mishka hasn't been using my design skills, and they're pretty rusty. I don't know if I'll be much help to you."

"Don't be silly! I loved all the stuff you did to your friend's place. It's incredibly difficult to design spaces for men. It seems like most of the color schemes are gray, brown, or black. I loved the way you brought color into his space. It looks really organic and not 'design-y'."

I blush. "Thanks, we had great fun putting it together. At first, I wasn't sure if Cristiano would be onboard with my plans, but after he got into the spirit of things, it was fun to put his home together. He's so cute. Do you know he has a photo album on Facebook with nothing but pictures of his condo?"

"I saw. It's obvious he's thrilled with what you did for him. He's been singing your praises online."

"Yeah, about that … I'm not sure I deserve all the kudos. It was just a few fabrics and knickknacks to liven up his place."

"Don't sell yourself short, a happy client is a repeat customer," Donda shifts Kennadie to her other hip. "I need to get Kennadie down for a nap. When I get back, I want to hear all about this Cristiano."

"I don't have much to say. Cristiano's just a client who hired me to design a suit, and somehow along the way, we accidentally became friends."

Donda winks at me. "Something about your story rings awfully familiar. Oh, wait … I know. Your brother rescued me from a car accident and — well you know the rest."

"Whoa! Slow down. Cristiano is just a really supportive friend I made in a moment of crisis. I have no idea where we might go from here. He lives in another state and has a life completely separate from me."

"It seems you guys have great chemistry. For you all to be able to decorate his place without coming unglued is a pretty big accomplishment. You should've seen the heated discussions Jaxson and I had over the bathroom vanity. That was only one room — I can imagine how heated it must've gotten when you were doing his whole house."

"I know! I was shocked too. I expected it to be much more difficult, but he seemed game to try anything I suggested. Unlike some people I work with, Cristiano wasn't very stubborn about sticking to the way things were. It was a nice change from the usual clients I encountered at Mishka Unlimited. I hope he shows the same flexibility when it comes to his outfit for Sports Heroes with Heart."

"You'll be fine. The suit you designed for him is phenomenal — even in its unfinished state. Most people don't think of men's clothes as beautiful, but his suit truly is."

"I feel like I'm about to throw up. I'm nervous because my work is going to be shown side by side with designers who have decades of experience. I'm not sure how to get a handle on my fear."

"What does Cristiano say?"

"I don't know. We haven't really talked about it yet. He is supposed to be here on Tuesday for his final fitting. So, I guess I have to figure out if I'm going to call myself a design house or just go by my name. I know from working these events, the reporters always want to know who designed each outfit. I need to figure out what to call myself, or it could get awkward for Cristiano."

"All the exposure will do wonders for you," Donda remarks with a huge grin. "It might even generate enough interest in your designs that you could launch a whole new business. That's how it worked for me. I got some unexpected TV exposure and built a new career for myself."

"This is my first big design project which doesn't involve earning a college degree. I doubt anyone will be interested in what I designed. Still, it has been a fun challenge. Cristiano is completely jazzed to discover he can actually move in his suit. I forget how much we take it for granted that clothing fits."

"Speak for yourself. I'm tall, and I can never find any pants or dresses which are long enough for me. Most of the dresses these days hit me high enough on the thigh they are more like a tunic."

"Okay, I'll put you on my list of things to do. Everyone should be able to dress in clothes which work for their body type. Just because you have impossibly long legs doesn't mean you should feel like you're walking around naked."

"I guess I should be happy your brother is still thrilled when I wear one of my short skirts."

I plug my ears. "I so did not need to know that about my big brother."

Donda laughs. "You sound like Gabriel. He doesn't want to know these things either."

I choke back a snort of laughter. "Do you blame him? No teenager wants to know their parents are having sex. It's just weird."

⸺◆⸺

Jaxson takes the plate from me after I finish rinsing it off. As he dries it, he says, "We really haven't had a chance to talk since you moved here. My schedule has been crazy."

"It's all right. I've been working hard too. Don't sweat it."

"Donda told me about your new venture. She is excited about your design work. I think she has a bunch of outfits in mind for you to make."

"I love making clothes for you guys, but I also need to find myself a job. I can't be a freeloader forever."

"Jordie, don't worry about it. This house is huge, and we have more room than we could ever use. Having someone else knocking around in this big space is nice. I know Donda gets frustrated and lonely. I'm at the bottom of the totem pole and always pull the worst schedules. You're actually making me feel a little less guilty."

I heave a big sigh. "I'm lucky you or your wife want anything to do with me. If I haven't dropped an apology bomb on you recently, consider it done. You have no idea how much I wish I could go back and rewrite history."

"We told you not to worry about it," Jaxson puts his hands on my shoulders and angles me toward him. "If you want to know the real truth, I'm not sure I would change anything. Your attack on Donda actually brought us closer in the end. We had to talk some things through, but it all worked out."

I grimace. "No thanks to me. I still feel awful."

"Jordie, you need to forgive yourself. After all, you totally redeemed yourself at our wedding. If you hadn't done what you did, Donda would've been destroyed. So, all is forgiven."

I look at my brother with open skepticism as I ask, "Really?"

Jaxson examines me carefully. "Absolutely. Donda and I have had lots of things between us we've had to work through and around. A lot of them have to do with forgiving ourselves for what we did or didn't do in the past. We're not going to hold on to some silly grudge over things you said when you had a little too much to drink. Life is too short."

I put the saucepan down that I'm washing and dry my hands on a dish towel. I walk up to my brother and hug him around the waist. "I have missed you so much. You've always been my biggest fan and willing to forgive me almost everything. I need that in my life right about now."

Jaxson moves my hair out of my face. "How are

you doing? Things haven't been so great for you lately."

I grab my iced tea and walk over to the kitchen table and sit down before I answer, "I don't know. I know it sounds weird, but I can't tell how I'm doing. It changes from minute to minute. I feel lost. I don't think I've been without a job since I was in high school. As bad as it was at Mishka Unlimited, at least I had a sense of who I was."

Jaxson pulls out a chair and sits down. "It's so strange that Mishka is acting like you were not a huge part of her success. I remember when Mom was recovering and you wanted to stay here longer. I talked to Mishka on the phone back then, and she made it sound like you were indispensable to her business."

I shrug. "I don't know if I was irreplaceable or if Mishka just didn't want to pay me for the vacation time I had earned."

Jaxson scowls at me. "Don't undersell yourself. Before you started working for Mishka, she was some unknown design student. Whatever career she's had, you helped her build."

I fiddle around with the lemon in my tea as I say, "Even though I know you are right, it doesn't feel that way at the moment. It feels like I went away to New York and accomplished absolutely nothing — except, now I have a bad reference on my resume."

Jaxson raises his eyebrow. "I don't suppose you can chalk it up to artistic temperament?"

I snicker. "You might have a point. It wasn't this way at the beginning of her career, but lately, Mishka has been next to impossible for anyone to deal with. I spent most of my time on the phone apologizing to agents and suppliers. Some of them have started calling me 'The Beast Tamer'."

Jaxson laughs out loud. "Even you have to appreciate the irony."

I stick my tongue out at him "Oh … come on. I'm not quite that bad." I pause for a moment before I add, "Okay, I guess you're right — I am that bad. I'm working on it though. I don't suffer fools well. — especially when I'm the one who's making a fool out of myself."

"I chalk it up to the fact that you've always had lots of passion. I don't think there's ever been a topic between us which we actually see eye to eye on."

"Sometimes, my passion gets me in trouble."

Jaxson takes a long drink of his coffee before he responds, "From what my wife tells me, your career move might not necessarily have been something detrimental to you. Didn't you pick up a high-profile client? I know you haven't been happy at Mishka's for a while. So, maybe your argument with her was just the push you needed to succeed on your own."

Gabriel rushes into the kitchen. My nephew doesn't look very much like a child these days. Honestly, he looks like he could model menswear. Surprisingly, even though my brother is only his stepfather, they look and talk a lot alike.

"What's your fire?" Jaxson gives his stepson, Gabriel, the evil eye. "You know running in the house sets a bad example for your little sister."

"Aunt Jordan is on TV," he responds breathlessly.

Startled, I stand up and walk toward the living

room. "I don't know why I would be on television —"

As soon as I turn the corner and catch a glimpse at the TV, it all becomes clear. There, on my brother's flat screen TV is my former boss, bigger than life. The closed captioning is on so I can see what she's saying. Even printed out in small letters scrolling across the screen, what she is saying is horrifying. Gabriel doesn't even try to read the captioning, he just walks over to the TV and grabs the remote and turns up the volume.

"… It was just so tragic, I never expected someone I had known as long as Jordan Shepherd to steal all of my designs. I worked for hundreds of hours on each of those designs, and now she's stolen them to enrich herself." I watch with morbid fascination.

The interviewer is nodding eagerly and sympathetically. "I can't imagine the betrayal. After all, you created Jordan Shepherd from nothing."

I bristle at the description. "I might've been naïve and stupid, but I was never nothing! I don't know what Mishka's talking about. I took nothing from her business. I left everything I owned there — except family pictures. Stupidly, I even left my own stuff behind. I'm not sure what I was thinking. That's the kind of word vomit I used to get from her every day."

"Some people aren't very smart," my brother offers.

"You have a kabillion and a half years of schooling, and that's the best you can come up with, Dr. Shepherd?" I snap.

Jaxson puts his coffee cup up to his lips and takes a long drink. He shrugs. "You didn't tell me you wanted me to come up with something brilliant. I thought I was just listening to you tell me about your rotten couple of months."

I slump down in the kitchen chair. "Oh, my gosh! I'm going to have to tell Cristiano about this. He can't mention my name on the red carpet after this. It would hurt more than help."

Jaxson comes and sits beside me on the couch. He puts his arm around my shoulder. "I'm not a media genius or anything, but here's what we learned when we tried to share Donda's story. Conflict and controversy make people pay attention. I guess it's human nature to be interested in the drama around us. I know it's painful now, but in the long run, this might do wonders for your career. Mishka is the one who has made a grave mistake."

"What if people don't believe me when I explain I didn't steal anything from her?" I ask, feeling desperate. "For a moment, I thought everything would start going my way, and now this feels like a huge slap in the face."

Gabriel is studying something on his tablet. He looks up at me. "Someone stole my comic book designs once. He was using some sketches I put up on a gaming board, and he was claiming he drew them. Other than the fact that they were originally posted under my account, I couldn't prove they were mine. I didn't take any screenshots or anything."

"Oh man, that sucks. I'm sorry," I commiserate.

Gabriel shrugs. "It did for a while. Eventually, the scammer had to put his money where his mouth was and produce other drawings. Soon enough, my boss figured out the dude couldn't even draw stick figures — and my online friends pointed him to me."

"That's cool. I'm glad you got the credit you deserve," I comment. "Wouldn't it be bizarre if that's what's happening with Mishka? I mean, I guess it's possible. She claims she works at night when no one else is around. I wonder if she's claiming credit for other people's work."

"Anything is possible. Look at Milli Vanilli," Gabriel adds.

My brother glances over at me. "I guess people will soon find out if she's the real deal. She has to replace you. That's won't be an easy feat. You were easily doing the work of about three people."

"I don't know what I think about Mishka. Back in the early days, she was a decent person. I don't know what happened. Part of me is cheering for her to be busted, the other part of me is sad it's come to this. I guess the kindest thing you can say about me is I'm thoroughly confused."

Gabriel shakes his head at me. "I think you're just a really nice person and you don't want to see bad things happen to your friend."

I shoot a playful stare at Gabriel. "Stop with the 'nice' stuff. You'll ruin my reputation for being a rabble-rouser. I am a terribly mean person, everyone knows it."

"Un-huh," Gabriel says in a doubtful tone, "I suppose you are being mean when you put away money in my college fund every single month."

I have to catch my breath. I thought I had hidden my tracks, but I guess someone noticed. "I can be mean and still be the cool, helpful aunt," I protest.

"Whatever you say, Aunt Jordan. I still think you're pretty nice."

CHAPTER EIGHT

CRISTIANO

A TRICKLE OF SWEAT slides down my back. My breath comes faster as I watch the scene unfold on Jubilee's phone. "That's a lie! I was there. I saw what happened. I can't believe she's going to get away with this!"

"I'm sorry, Cris," Jubilee answers. "I didn't mean to upset you. I thought you'd want to know. It sounds like you two are getting pretty serious." She gently removes the phone from my hands.

For a moment, I consider arguing with Jubilee about the state of my relationship with Jordan. Then it occurs to me; I'm not really sure where we left things either.

"I'm not upset with you — it's this whole situation," I clarify when I see Jubilee's crestfallen expression. "I only spent a couple hours with this Mishka chick, but I can tell you what she's saying about Jordan is false. I don't know why Mishka has it in for Jordan, but apparently, she does."

"It's hard when someone you care about is being attacked, but you haven't known Jordan very long —

there might be more to the story." Jubilee walks over to our beverage cooler in the corner of Rowden's office and pulls out a soda for me. "Have you eaten today?" Jubilee asks, slipping into her usual mothering mode.

"I'll grab something on the way home. I'm trying to finish up these revisions Rowden wanted. Does he know the sound wasn't working on our shoot? I can only hear about every other word of the interview," I roll my shoulders to work out the knots. "I'll have to do a lot of voiceover segments to make this story work. We need to put more money into equipment for the field."

Jubilee shrugs. "You know Rowden, he's trying to run this whole thing on a shoestring budget."

I swipe my hand through my hair. "I get that, but I still need the tools to make all this work. If we can't hear the athletes we're interviewing, there's no point in us doing field shoots. We should just do the commentary on pool footage from each sport."

"You're preaching to the choir. I've told Rowden over and over again we need more to be able to compete with the big boys. But, that's not how he thinks, so we'll have to adjust."

"Speaking of adjusting, has Rowden talked to you about the name of our show?" I ask.

"Why?" Jubilee looks a little crestfallen. "Xyresic is such a cool word."

"Yeah, if you play Scrabble; but it doesn't work for the name of a sports show. I think that's part of the reason they keep bumping us back into the middle of the night on the schedule. We're not getting good name recognition and a sustainable fan base. I think a name change would help."

Jubilee nods slightly. "That makes sense. Why haven't you guys made the change?"

I place my hand over my mouth as I try to swallow a chuckle. "Your husband seems to think you would be horribly offended if we changed it."

She shakes her head vigorously. "Oh Geez, that man drives me crazy sometimes. All I said is that it would make a good title for a book or something. I never intended for him to name a sports show after my favorite word. I'm not that weird." I raise my eyebrow at her as I take in her tie-dye bandanna and studded halter top. "Hopefully, you can talk to Rowden and tell him you're not married to the show name, only to him."

Jubilee stands on her tiptoes and kisses me on the cheek. "Don't worry Cris, I'll sort it out."

"Thanks. You probably hold more sway over him than I do. He trusts your opinion."

"Speaking of trust, what are you going to do about your girlfriend? You know, she's gonna need you more now than ever."

"Let's hope I'm overreacting and this doesn't turn into anything huge. Jordan's life is in enough of an upheaval right now anyway. I hate to have to tell her about this and make her relive every decision she's made recently."

"I saw her boss on YouTube, I can see why she left her job. It would've been absolutely certifiably nuts for her to stay there. That lady is like pure venom."

"Mishka Silk is rude to anybody and everybody

whenever she has a chance. I'm glad Jordan is clear across the country from Mishka's poisonous garbage."

"I've learned the hard way that when you are an Internet sensation, even if the reasons are good, people don't know how to treat you properly afterwards."

"Hopefully, this is all overblown, and Mishka will move on to bigger and better things."

"She could, but I wouldn't bet on it." Jubilee frowns.

I start to twirl a pencil in my fingers. "How do I help Jordan rebuild her life when she doesn't fully believe in her own talent — especially when someone is publicly tearing her down?"

"You need to start by showing her one day at a time that she is more important to you than anything she could create," Jubilee advises.

"How do I do that without making it seem like I don't value her art?" I asked trying to sort out Jubilee's words.

Jubilee reaches out and pats my arm. "I'm sorry, I don't have any perfect advice for you. It is a dance you guys need to work out between the two of you."

I sigh. "I'm afraid she'll decide she regrets the day she met me — she probably wishes she could go back to the way it was before. I don't think I'm all right with that, she means too much to me."

"Then you have to find a way to tell her how you feel — sooner rather than later — because whatever is going on public-relations-wise is going to shake her confidence. She needs to know you'll be there for her, no matter what."

———— ◆ ————

As Jordan smooths out the back of my new jacket, I keep my gaze trained on her window. As tempted as I am to look, I don't want to ruin her big reveal. I'm spending so much time in Oregon these days it's starting to feel more like home than Aspen.

Jordan reaches up, grasps my shoulders and turns me slightly. "Okay, you can look now. Be honest, I need to know what you really think."

I stare at myself in the mirror hanging on the back of Jordan's bedroom door in utter astonishment. It's the first time since junior high I look normal in dress clothes. Usually, I feel like an overstuffed piñata. I move my arms around in a pretend golf swing as I say, "I don't golf, but I totally could. In fact, I could probably ride my bike in this thing. Jordan, you are phenomenal."

"Thanks. I was hoping you would like it," she says as she examines me critically. "Looks like I need to shorten your left sleeve about a quarter of an inch."

"Really? I can finally move, twist and turn — and you're worried about a quarter of an inch? I wouldn't even worry about it. You should've seen what I had to wear before."

"I've seen some of this stuff you've worn before. You are a tad popular on social media. There are plenty of opportunities to see your fashion choices. You always look very handsome — but also very uncomfortable."

"After this, I'm not going to buy off the rack ever again. This is beyond cool."

"Speaking of cool, since you'll be in Southern California in the middle of summer, I chose a breathable fabric for your suit. Hopefully, you won't pass out from heat stroke while you stand on the red carpet."

"I didn't even think about the weather. Thanks for considering that. I would hate to dissolve into a puddle of sweat."

Jordan's doorbell rings and the little puppy goes crazy. He is barking as if he's some sort of Rottweiler. Jordan sets her sewing pins down, walks over to the door and opens it. From where I'm standing, I can't see who it is, but I hear him say, "Have a nice day ma'am, you've been served."

My stomach tightens. Nothing good ever comes from those words. The thought of Jordan having to go to court makes me nauseous.

Jordan clears her throat before she mumbles, "Oh, okay, thank you."

"What was that about?" I watch her close the door and slump against it. She is holding a thick envelope and her hands are shaking. I walk over and place my arm around her shoulders. "Whatever it is, we'll deal with it." I kiss her temple and brush a tear from her cheek with the pad of my thumb.

Jordan opens the envelope with trembling fingers. After she takes a moment to scan the documents, she sighs as more tears escape. "I can't believe she actually did it. How in the world does she expect me to fight this? I'm living on my brother's hide-a-bed. What am I supposed to do now?"

Trying to tamp down my anger over the situation, I

walk Jordan over to the couch and pull her down beside me. "Lots of people threaten to file lawsuits and never follow through. It might not be serious."

Jordan looks at me with a raised eyebrow. "Does Mishka strike you as someone who doesn't take things seriously? I think she's probably deadly serious."

I let out the breath I have been unconsciously holding. "You're right. Mishka probably isn't a practical joker. However, just because she can file suit, it doesn't mean she should. She may not have a single legal leg to stand on."

"See, in the world of make-believe that is fashion, it doesn't matter who's telling the truth. It only matters how many fans you have and who hires you to make them beautiful. There are so many people trying to get in Mishka's good graces, it's hard to say what they might say to get on her good side."

I hang my head and rub the back of my neck. "I've been in a situation like that before — I know it's no fun."

"You were in the middle of a girl fight in a design studio?" Jordan asks with a watery grin.

"Not exactly," I grimace. "When I was still racing BMX, it seemed I got too big for someone else's comfort. So, they devised a scheme to take me down. They were almost successful."

Jordan reaches out and grabs my hand and squeezes. "I'm sorry. What happened?"

"I thought I was invincible. I was at the top of my game. What could possibly touch me?" I stand, and pace around the room. "It wasn't long before one of my competitors took advantage of my carelessness. His plan was to remove me from the sport so he could advance."

"How awful!" Jordan exclaims. Her brows are furrowed with concern.

"Yeah, it got grisly there for a while. Maddox hired a cheerleader from one of the high schools in the area and had her claim we'd been partying and I gave her alcohol and drugs. This was a huge deal to my sponsors. One of my sponsors was a soap company. They made their money on my image as the boy next door. All the false accusations almost got me kicked out of racing altogether and cost several thousand dollars in endorsement deals."

"Did she have the brains to back off when you could refute her story?"

I shake my head. "She dug in a little harder and up the ante by claiming I forced her into sexual activity with not only myself but my teammates."

"Why would she do such a thing?" Jordan asks with a horrified expression.

"The only thing I've come up with is that Maddox was paying her and she could. I think it gave her a sense of power to hold my career in her hands."

Jordan squeezes my hand tighter. "How did things turn out?"

"Fortunately for me, we live in a time when everyone has a camera pointed at you at all times. There were several motocross fans in the bar that night where the partying supposedly took place. The videos showed I was not even there. I say *that night* because I considered the guys involved to be my friends and I could've just as easily been with them."

"Even if you had been with them, you wouldn't have been hitting on some high school girl. I haven't known you very long, but you're a stand-up guy."

"Making someone else do things without their permission is a hard line for me. When I first entered the racing circuit, I was a green teenager whose voice hadn't even changed, but several racing veterans took me under their wing and told me never to mess with my fans. I never forgot their advice as I grew older."

"Did you even know the girl who was lobbing accusations at you?"

Grimly, I shake my head. "No, the first time I ever saw her she was on the news telling people I had given her Ecstasy. I started much too young and I drank far more than was healthy in those days. But, I never touched drugs."

"I'm so sorry that happened to you. It must have been horrible."

"It was grueling — but, what's happening to you isn't fair either. People like that should have a special place in hell. You can't ruin someone's life for no reason, it's just wrong. We're going to do everything in our power, so Mishka doesn't ruin your life."

"You never told me what happened to the piece of garbage who was pointing the finger at you."

I shrug. "Her case was dismissed for lack of evidence, and her parents tried to come after me. It was touch and go there for a while. Eventually, the truth won out, and the jury believed me."

"I bet having those videotapes helped your case a lot."

"They pretty much saved me from prison. A lot of people gripe about all the social media in our lives; I thank God for it every day. If it hadn't been for people who wanted to show off for their friends and post videos on the Internet, I might not have had the evidence I needed to prove my innocence."

I lean over and kiss her on the forehead. "I believe the same concept applies here — eventually, Mishka will have to put up or shut up. We both know she doesn't have anything to put up."

Jordan throws her arms around my neck. "You'll never know how much it means to me that you are fighting for me." I am taken completely off guard when Jordan pulls my face down to hers and gives me a sultry kiss.

When I break off the kiss and pull away. I have to take a deep breath to steady my heart. That's the best kiss I've ever had. It's all I can do not to go back for more. "Wow! If that's the way you say thank you, you can thank me every single day."

Jordan hides her face. "I'm sorry. Sometimes, I feel so alone — it's nice to think about you fighting side-by-side with me to show Mishka that she does not have all the power."

I nod my head. "That's exactly what we'll do. Mishka only thinks she's the head of the universe — we will prove otherwise."

CHAPTER NINE

JORDAN

As I struggle with the button on my blue jeans, I continue to berate myself. I don't know what I was thinking. Why would I do something as stupid as kissing the guy who hired me for my first real job as a designer? Sure, Cristiano is cute and smart *and* funny *and* loyal — but, he's also my client. I don't know what possessed me to grab him and pull him into a lip lock. That was probably the single dumbest thing I've done in my whole entire career — at least since my boyfriend and I were caught making out in the delivery car when I worked at a pizza place.

I wrestle my shoe away from Brando. At the moment, the puppy is climbing into my lap and tackling my shoelace as if it is a vicious snake. I haven't had a dog since I was a kid. I've forgotten how much I miss them. I can't wait to have my own place, so I have the space for a pet.

After I get my shoes on, I walk over to the old-fashioned vanity Donda has placed in my room. It's cute

— not my style — but cute. I pick up a brush and pull my hair back into a ponytail. I am startled to see the panicked look on my face.

I know kissing Cristiano was not a brilliant move, but it was oh so nice. I need to focus. I'm working with Donda's difficult client today, so I need to be on my 'A game.' Thinking about the kiss that shouldn't have been is not the way to get focused. Even as I argue with myself, part of me wonders; what's the worst that could happen if I move forward with this relationship with Cristiano. Guys don't come much nicer than him. Our brief kiss was the most chemistry I felt with anyone in a long time. I'm tempted to forget professionalism and take the path which leads to immediate gratification.

Donda yells up the stairs, "Are you ready to go?"

"I'll be down in a minute," I respond.

"Bring the puppy down with you," Donda replies. When I reach the bottom of the stairs, Donda asks, "Are you ready for this?" Donda hands me a tie-dyed baseball cap with her logo on it.

"These are clever — who made these?"

"I had a little fun with my niece the other day. Becca is really artistic. When I do tie-dye, I usually end up with ugly grayish brown splotches; but hers are crisp, clean and colorful. Just don't tell anybody I'm using her for artistic inspiration."

"What? Not everybody uses third-graders to promote their business?" I try to hide my grin. "You're sure your client won't be upset if you bring someone else with you?"

"I warned her in advance. We're at an impasse — she wants new designs, and I had my heart set on the ones I've already drawn up."

"Okay, I think I can work with that." Fear gathers in my chest. I take a couple of calming breaths and remind myself I made a fair amount of money in college by making over people's homes. They all seemed pleased with the result. I suppose I don't really have anything to worry about, I have the experience and the education. Lord knows, after working for Mishka, I have excellent customer service skills. I have spent more than my fair share of time smoothing over ruffled feathers.

"Who are we working with?" I ask with some trepidation.

"I don't know if Madison told you this, but she works at a lifestyle magazine which focuses on the music scene and all that accompanies it."

"Really? I hadn't heard. I figured she would go back to writing about the criminal justice system and crimes which aren't typically picked up by media."

"She still works on cold cases as a hobby. She decided after having her daughter she wanted to lay off the grisly stuff while her kiddo was still young."

I put Brando down and throw the little squeaky toy at his feet. I smile as he does a belly-flop when he dives for the toy. Brando scampers back toward me dragging a bone nearly as big as he is. I chuckle. "You are such a silly little bruiser," I exclaim as I pick him up and give him a kiss. I walk him over to the kennel and place him inside as I say, "Be good until we get back. I'll play some more with you later."

Donda clicks her tongue. "It's too bad you don't want to be a mom. You are a natural. It's a waste of talent."

I sigh as I place the baseball cap on my head and thread my ponytail through the back. "I can have a great life without kids. Children are not everything."

Donda shakes her head in dismay as she comments, "I just don't understand that. My kids are my everything. I can't imagine my life without them."

My heart sinks at the implicit criticism. Frustrated, I place my hands on my hips. "It's not like I decided to have a kid and drop him off at the pound or something. I have the right to make my own decisions, and I'm making the choice not to become a parent. That doesn't make me a bad person, it just means I want different things in my life. Motherhood is not the only path to happiness."

"How do you know you wouldn't like being a mom? It might be the thing which makes you the happiest," Donda insists.

I level an angry glance at her. "And it might not. If I say I'm not cut out for motherhood, there's probably a reason behind it. I'm asking you to respect my choice."

Donda sets down her portfolio and purse as she comes over to give me a hug. "I can do that. Lord knows, I'm in no position to judge anyone else's life choices." As she picks up her belongings and heads out the door, she says over her shoulder, "I'm sorry, I didn't mean hurt your feelings."

I shrug. "No harm done." I place my purse on the floor by my feet and buckle in. "Now, tell me about Mrs.

Llewellyn —"

"Are you sure you want me to?" Donda asks.

"Yes, otherwise I wouldn't have asked," I answer with a chuckle.

"As it so happens, Kitty Llewellyn is a huge fan of Mishka Silk," Donda responds with an eye roll.

"Interesting, I wonder if it'll work in our favor."

Donda grimaces. "I guess it depends on how much gossip she listens to."

"That's what I'm afraid of. It doesn't seem so much like gossip when it comes directly from Mishka's mouth. Apparently, it doesn't matter if she tells the truth. The simple, plain, and boring truth doesn't sell television spots and magazines."

"Have you spoken to my brother, Jeff, about this? Maybe he can tell you what your options are."

I flinch. "I'd rather not face the reality that this whole spat with Mishka might be serious enough that I need to hire an attorney — especially since I can't afford to pay one. Moving across the country and paying a fee to get out of my lease pretty much wiped out all of my savings."

"I don't think my brother would charge you. After all, you're family now."

"When I was in New York, I was so detached from everything on this coast it's hard to feel like I'm one of the family."

Donda reaches across the car and squeezes my arm. "Don't worry. We'll catch you up. We just need to have a meeting of the Girlfriend Posse."

"I don't know. The prospect of seeing everyone makes me nervous. I made such a fool out of myself the last time I was with your friends. It might be more than a little awkward," I admit.

"It's okay. It's not the first time one of us has made a mistake, and it won't be the last. It seems to me you could use some people behind you."

"You can say that again — but, how will the Girlfriend Posse help me talk to Jeff?"

"I guess I forgot to mention it. We're having dinner at my mom's house Saturday. You're invited along with everyone else in the gang. Denny is making his famous chili. If there is something that needs to be dealt with which requires the Girlfriend Posse, the guys are used to the way we work, and they'll make themselves scarce."

"The way you guys stand up for each other is awe-inspiring. If they are willing to, I definitely could use some reinforcements."

"Jordan, all you had to do was ask," Donda responds.

"I'm not very good at asking, but I'll try to remember." I try to keep the emotion out of my voice. I can't believe I ever thought Donda was bad for my brother. She's a godsend.

⬤

"Do you miss New York? What is it like to be back home?" Mindy asks.

"It is a little strange to be back in Oregon," I admit. "Things seem to move at a different pace here.

Everything is a little less frantic."

As if to demonstrate my point, Aidan and Tyler are sitting around the fire pit picking out songs on their guitar. Denny and Gwendolyn are attempting to dance. Tara, Madison, and Heather are helping the younger kids up Aidan's rock climbing apparatus. Yes, the pace here is very much different from New York. I could get used to this.

"Do you miss your job?" Mindy's question makes me pause for a moment.

"There are certain things I miss. I like Fashion Week, and all the other people I worked with when helping Mishka put together a show. That kind of excitement can be a little addicting even though I was only a small part of it."

Donda hands me an iced tea when she sits down beside me. "Don't let her fool you. Jordan has the magic touch with clients. At first, my client was a little bit skeptical of Jordan's abilities. Apparently, she had seen the article in the tabloids and didn't know what to believe. By the time we were done, she was singing Jordan's praises. Trust me, this lady is a tough nut to crack. I've done five sets of designs for her, and she wasn't pleased with any of them. Jordan talked to her for a few moments and made a sketch, and the client was head over heels in love with it."

"Don't be too impressed," I caution, waving off the praise. "I just happen to know someone who has her design aesthetic."

Donda snickers. "Yeah, I noticed … Better Homes & Gardens, 1985 called. They'd like their design back."

I shrug helplessly. "It's my job as a designer to try to meet the client's needs. If she was stuck in the eighties, that's where I have to go."

"I am surprised you were able to read her so quickly. By looking at her, I would not have guessed the nostalgia factor. She dresses like a fashion model. Who knew she wanted white stained oak in her kitchen? I don't even know how you came up with it."

"Well, I spent about ten minutes talking to her about inconsequential things. She mentioned over and over about her daughter dying of cancer in 1986 and that her life has never been the same. She told me she wished things could go back to the way they were. I played a hunch — I figured she might want her house to look the way it did before too," I explain.

"That was pretty smart," Mindy responds. "Although it's a bummer she believes everything she reads in the tabloids."

"Trust me, I wish I could stop Mishka from saying things that are not true. I don't know if there's anything I can do about it."

Mindy's father, Jeff, responds, "Actually, there are some things you could do, but I don't know if they would be productive. Still, you might want to look into counter-suing her."

"What in the world could I sue her for? She's claiming I stole all of her designs. What power do I have to prove I didn't?"

Gabriel looks up from his iPad as he says, "I'm not a lawyer like Uncle Jeff — but I think it would depend on how you develop your designs."

"I don't know if any of it matters," I admit with a tired sigh.

"Oh, it matters. If you've done any of your design work on the computer, it wouldn't be hard to rebuild your history to show what happened."

"I have a habit of drawing my drawings on paper and then scanning them into the computer so I can paint them with the computer program using different fabrics and textures."

"I think you can probably take a deep breath and relax. It means you should have computer files for everything you design which date back to the moment you conceived the idea."

"That's good to hear, but I don't know if Mishka is going to roll over quite so easily."

"Could you get Cristiano to sign an affidavit or something explaining what he saw that day?" Aidan suggests.

"He's already offered — but I hate to drag him down with me."

Aidan shrugs. "I know courtrooms are scary. But, so is letting her be the only voice in the atmosphere. I think you need to punch back."

"You think it would be worth it?" I ask, eager for Jeff's legal opinion on the matter.

Jeff gives an almost imperceptible roll of his shoulder. "I don't know, there are risks either way. However, it's worth exploring, for sure. Why don't you bring any paperwork you have with you the next time you come over?"

"Okay, I can do that. I don't want to ruin this family dinner with talk of my epically failing career. I would like to explore my options though. I appreciate your help."

"You're a member of the Girlfriend Posse. My wife would kill me if I didn't at least try to help you."

"That doesn't change the fact I'm exceptionally grateful for your help."

Jeff shrugs. "It's just what we do around here."

⸺•⸺

Using my foot, I rock the swing on Gwendolyn's front porch as I try to follow the conversation of the women who are with me. It is clear the friendships in this group are deep and abiding, despite the differences in ages. Every time I watch the Girlfriend Posse in action, I'm left a little speechless. This is one powerful group of women. Started by best friends Kiera, Tara and Heather, this group always have each other's back. Although the composition of the group has changed over the years as Kiera and Jeff's circle of friends grows, the spirit remains the same.

Tonight is no exception. Mindy is explaining her anxiety over taking the SAT to get into college, and everyone else is sharing their experiences and how they overcame the challenge of standardized entrance exams. College seems like a lifetime ago. I barely remember the process of getting in.

I'm busy people watching when suddenly Gwendolyn addresses me, "Jordan, you've been quiet. Why don't you tell us about your handsome beau?"

"Way to get to the point, Mom," Donda remarks

with a laugh.

"Can you blame me for being curious?" Gwendolyn counters.

I blush. "There isn't much to tell. Cristiano isn't my beau. I am just designing a suit for him."

Kiera chuckles softly. "You're not fooling anyone. Your face lights up like a beacon when you talk about him. It seems to me, there might be something else going on."

My gaze shifts to the ground. "No, not really —"

Madison opens up a juice box for her daughter before she comments, "I suspect there might not be anything at this moment, but you'd like there to be."

I blush even deeper. "Have you guys met Cristiano? He's about as perfect as I'm going to find. Unfortunately, he's also my client — and that makes things awkward."

Madison slaps my knee playfully. "You don't have to worry about any of us judging you. I think about half of us met our spouses through our jobs."

Kiera nods vigorously. "Madison's right. I met Jeff when he was on lifeguarding duty, and I rescued a little boy."

"Even though Tyler is one of Jeff's best friends, things didn't get serious between us until after he investigated a gunshot incident at my food truck," adds Heather.

"I might fit this category too," comments Tara. "I fell in love with Aidan as a teenager, but we lost track of each other, and when we found each other, he was playing the piano at Kiera's wedding."

I look at all the women in the group, and they are smiling. "So ... what you're saying is the crush I am experiencing isn't unusual?"

"I say go for it," Donda remarks.

"Really?" I ask wistfully. "He is a great guy. I could use someone like him in my life. I haven't slept much in the last few days because I was worried I'd overstepped my bounds."

"What'd you do?" Mindy's eyes widen.

Feeling a little shaky, I confess, "I don't know if I should be telling you this, but we shared a really hot kiss. It was like our chemistry was off the charts."

Mindy giggles. "Is that all? It just means you are like my mom and dad. They still kiss like they're newlyweds. It's embarrassing to take them anywhere in public."

Kiera tweaks her daughter's hair. "Oh hush! Just wait until it happens to you —"

"I know, you keep saying that. I don't know..." Mindy responds with a somber look.

"You all don't think it's weird?" I press. "What if he doesn't want what I want?"

Gwendolyn shakes her head. "I say, if you like your young man and he pushes all of your buttons, you need to explore what that's all about. What could be the harm?"

"He really does push all my buttons in the best of ways."

"Well, that settles it. Let me know if you want a place to go when Cristiano is in town. There's this little Italian place down from my florist shop which is perfect for dates. It's very romantic."

"Thank you, Gwendolyn. I'll keep it in mind if I get brave enough to make a move."

"I'm sure you will," Donda remarks. "Jaxson always says you are the most fearless between the two of you. You can do this. You have the support of the whole Girlfriend Posse if you get nervous."

"I don't know … given the history of this group, that could be a scary thing," I joke. "You all may be planning my wedding before we actually go out on a date."

Gwendolyn laughs out loud. "I can't say you're wrong. This group is a big believer in romance."

CHAPTER TEN

CRISTIANO

"ARE YOU READY FOR this?" I ask Jordan.

She clutches my hand. "I don't know. I've been on red carpets before, but I've never been front and center."

Jordan's excitement and fear is a tangible thing. This is the first time I have ever attended one of these events with someone I care about. It's an entirely different experience. I feel fiercely protective of Jordan. I want this to be the most magical night she's ever had.

I lean down and kiss her temple. "Just take a deep breath. I used to feel this way before every single race. Don't worry, you'll kill it. My new suit by JS Couture is the best looking one here. I have no doubt people will fall in love with you and your designs," I respond, trying to calm her nerves. Still, her hand is shaking and ice cold inside mine.

"You can be glad Sports Heroes with Heart is a worthy charity. If it wasn't, I would be at home cowering under my favorite blankie."

I squeeze her hand in reassurance. Jordan tilts forward and kisses me lightly on the bottom of my chin. "Thank you so much for trying to calm me down and distracting me. I'll be okay. This is just first-time jitters."

"If you want a real distraction, I can provide it." I wink.

"Don't give me a good reason to run away from this event — because I would in a heartbeat." Jordan grimaces.

The line around us moves forward. I whisper in her ear, "It's show time. You are going to rock it."

Jordan straightens my tie before we round the corner and are blinded by flashbulbs. She wobbles on her heels at the unexpected assault. I place my arm around her waist to steady her as I whisper, "Look away for a minute and blink your eyes. Eventually, you'll get used to it."

"I'm not sure I want to." Panic colors her voice. "I prefer being backstage."

"I gotcha," I say as we duck behind someone much more famous. Suddenly, we enter the recording space of a reporter I know from one of the TV magazine shows. He has interviewed me before and is a decent, fair guy.

"Hey, Cristiano! Congratulations on being recognized for your charity work. What do you have planned next?"

"Well, you know I got a little show on TV. We cover the X-Games."

"Your show has a weird name, but I watch *Xyresic* all the time. Do you have any big plans coming up?" he answers with a cheesy grin.

I return his smile. "It's great that you're a fan, I hope you continue to watch. We are proud of the work we do on *Xyresic*. We'll be covering more races and providing more in-depth interviews. We just upgraded our field equipment. You'll feel like you're right there racing."

"Good stuff, man." He turns to Jordan and asks, "Who is this lovely creature on your arm?"

My chest puffs up with pride. "This is Jordan from JS Couture. She created my outfit for this evening. Jordan wanted to make sure I gave Sports Heroes with Heart my best. Didn't she do a great job?"

The reporter stammers for a moment before he says, "Well, you know fashion isn't really my thing, but you look pretty dapper. Thanks for taking the time to speak to me, Cristiano. Good luck tonight."

A production assistant comes up and escorts Jordan and me down the carpet. "You did great. That gave us a lot of usable footage."

"It wasn't a problem, I've always liked your boss," I mumble as another set of flashes hit our eyes.

"I'll let you guys proceed. Thanks for the interview," she says as she ushers us around a couple who is stopped on the carpet posing for pictures.

"Boy, I'm glad it's over," Jordan whispers as she clutches my arm. "I never considered myself to be shy until tonight. This is overwhelming. It's a lot more fun to watch on television."

We stop and turn toward the crowd as a bright light floods the area. Apparently, we are going to be featured on live television. "The name is Cristiano Romero, and this is Jordan Shepherd from JS Couture," I tell the assistant making flashcards for the host.

"What do you hope to accomplish here tonight?" A female reporter asks as she shoves a mic in my face.

"This is an amazing cause which helps kids with disabilities be able to go to summer camp. A lot of times these kids don't get to take part in organized sports. Sports Heroes with Heart would like to give back and send more kids to camp," I explain, highlighting the evening's charitable purpose.

"Well, if that's not one of the sweetest things I've ever heard, I don't know what is. *Are You Gonna Wear That?!* is a fashion show at heart, even though we like to cover entertainment. Can you tell us who designed your suit? You look very rugged and manly — but put together," she gushes.

I point to Jordan. "My phenomenal suit was designed by the lovely Jordan Shepherd. She is the best designer I've ever met."

The reporter's eyebrows climb up to her hairline as she asks, "Isn't she the one who used to work for Mishka Silk? How do you know the design for your suit was not stolen from Mishka?"

"For one thing, I was there in Mishka's studio when Jordan left. She took nothing with her. I watched her design this suit piece by piece from a paper pattern to a muslin pattern and then to the design as a whole. I was part of the process every step of the way. Jordan did not steal anything from any other designer. This design came from Jordan's head as she tried to address my specific needs."

"Specific needs?" The reporter asks with a puzzled expression.

Jordan steps forward. "Yes, as you can see, Mr. Romero is a tall, handsome guy with wide shoulders. It is difficult for him to purchase clothes off the rack. I designed the suit to accentuate his best features and still be comfortable. It is my hope to do this for clients around the world. Everyone should have great clothes regardless of body size."

The reporter frowns at Jordan. "So, you are going to exclusively focus on couture clothing? What about our viewers who can't afford exorbitant fees?"

"I am at the beginning stages of forming JS Couture. I don't know what the ultimate form of my business will be. But it is my intent to make all of my clothing line as accessible as possible."

The reporter is silent for a moment and then asks Jordan, "Could you design something for people like me? I am so tiny that when I dress professionally, everything looks like I'm a kid playing dress-up in my mom's clothes. Everything hangs off my shoulders, and the sleeves are always too long."

Jordan nods sympathetically. "I might be able to work something out. After this is all over, come find me, and I'll give you my number."

The reporter suddenly remembers she's still on the air and says, "I guess I should let these folks go on their way because the event is starting soon, but I appreciate Jordan Shepherd's unique approach to fashion. I am sure we'll be hearing much more from JS Couture in the future."

Her assistant gives a signal to the cameraman, and he shuts out the camera and the lights for a moment. "I hope you do what you say you're going to do. There are so many of us who don't fall within the normal range. It makes it hard to buy anything."

"I'll do my best," Jordan says as she reaches into her tiny clutch purse and draws out a business card. "Give me a call."

"You didn't do any of those things Mishka is accusing you of, did you?" The reporter asks as she studies Jordan.

"No, I didn't," Jordan asserts simply.

"My gut feeling tells me you're telling the truth. Would you like to come on *Are You Gonna Wear That?!* and explain your side of the story?"

"I'm tempted because I don't like what Mishka is saying about me. It is wrong for her to lie, but going on TV and trashing her won't solve anything. It would only complicate matters. If it's all right with you, I'd rather showcase what I can do instead of complaining about another designer."

"How long before you would have your line put together? If you can do it before the end of September, I've got some empty slots available."

Jordan draws in a breath. "I can try. Can I use you as a model? Your problems are not uncommon. So, if I could design something around your body type with narrow shoulders, it would probably be marketable to lots of people."

"Will I get to keep the outfit?" the reporter presses.

Jordan smiles. "Of course. Why would I make clothes to fit you and then give them away to someone else?"

The reporter grins. "Consider me your next model. I would love to have you come on my show to showcase some fashion diversity."

"Okay, call me on Monday, and we'll figure the details out."

The reporter smiles and reaches out to shake Jordan's hand. "Thank you. By the way, my name is Aisha Francis."

Jordan shakes her hand and smiles. "I look forward to your call. It was a pleasure to meet you. I appreciate you highlighting the work I'm doing."

"Thank you. I hope this works out well for all of us. Have a lovely evening," I gently lead Jordan down the carpet. People are stacking up behind us and getting restless.

After we get away from the biggest throng of people, Jordan looks at me in shock as she asks, "Did I really just launch a whole fashion line on national television? Jeff is going to have a cow."

<hr />

Jordan feeds me a bite of popcorn as we sit on the couch and watch a replay of our red-carpet arrival and appearance on *Are You Gonna to Wear That?!* "I don't even resemble a biker. I've come so far. Because of you, I look like I belong in the big leagues."

Jordan smiles a small private smile. "I have to agree with you. That came across even better on TV than I expected. I love the colors in your tie. The color palette certainly brought out your eyes."

"It's like you guys are speaking in some secret code. I'm in the dark about that sort of stuff. Still, you picked up some buzz, Rowden should be happy."

"I am so glad. That means my mission was accomplished," Jordan comments as she takes a long drink of soda. "Oh, watch this! I almost fell down here because someone stepped on the back of my dress."

"I wondered why you suddenly grabbed me and wouldn't let go."

"Yeah, I have a habit of doing that with people I really like," she teases. She scoots closer and cuddles against my side.

I shift positions so she's reclining against me. "I'm so glad," I murmur against her hair.

"Me too," she whispers.

"I thought it was stupid when Rowden suggested I go see a designer, but I am so happy I ended up with you. By the way, your mission with me is not quite over. You told me if you developed a pattern, you would make me some more in different colors. You can't up and leave."

"I did say that. But, now I have other clients who have needs. You might have to wait in line."

I frown playfully. "I guess I can wait, I don't plan to go anywhere."

"You know, that might be my favorite thing to come out of this whole situation. Being threatened with a lawsuit from Mishka totally sucks, but the rest of this has worked out better than my wildest dreams."

"Karma can be like that," I murmur.

"Yeah, and ... guess what? Karma means I ran out of space on my answering machine and in my inbox. There are so many people contacting me with special needs — I have lost count of them all."

"Sounds like you have found a niche market."

"I have you to thank. If you hadn't challenged me to go outside of my comfort zone, I probably wouldn't have done this."

"I don't know that I actually did all that. All I wanted was a suit which fit."

"Well, whether it was on purpose or by accident, it has launched me on a different path. Thank you so much for being supportive."

"There isn't anywhere else I'd rather be."

CHAPTER ELEVEN

JORDAN

AISHA EXAMINES MY PROJECT boards with a keen eye. "What do you have going on here?"

"Too many things to count!" I confess. "The top row is variations of the suit you saw Cristiano wearing at the event. I am making one in blue —"

"Oh, it'll look so good with his eyes. I'm a little jealous that you get to use a guy like Cristiano as a living mannequin," she replies as she winks.

I can't help but laugh at her suggestive statement. "Cristiano is definitely the most unusual dress form I've ever worked with."

"I bet. What's the other one?" she asks with open curiosity.

"I'm working on adapting my muslin pattern to casual wear. It's not only suits which cause problems. I'm making him a more casual jacket for when he works out in the field covering races."

"Will you be able to do the same thing for me? Once you figure out what size I am, can you replicate the pattern?"

I nod. "That's the plan. I want to find what works for you. Once we do, we can adapt your pattern for many different uses."

"Wow, I'm so glad my brother is a motocross fan. If it weren't for him, I wouldn't have known who Cristiano was. I ended up getting a great interview and a solution to all my wardrobe problems."

I put a tape measure on her arm. "Bend your arm please," I instruct as I write down a series of numbers.

"What's the rest of this stuff?" Aisha asks, pointing to the board.

"Well, the second row is for my sister-in-law who has a very short waist and legs which seem a mile and a half long. She has the hardest time finding clothes. She often wears men's pants because she can choose the length."

"There's nothing more humiliating than having to wear clothes which aren't the style you would like to wear. Pretty soon you start to feel like there's something wrong with your body."

"I agree. I love unusual clothes, and I could never find any which didn't look like a teenager should be wearing them. That's one of the reasons I chose a career in fashion design." I measure her waist.

Putting my tools down, I hand her a book as fabric samples. "Let me know what you think of these and your favorite colors. I'll develop a color palette which works for you."

Aisha does a happy little dance. "I can't remember the last time I was excited about the prospect of new clothes. You're brilliant!"

"Well, I am just starting out. I don't know how successful I'll be in the long run. People might not like my design aesthetic."

Aisha clicks her tongue at me. "From what I've seen, your taste is spot on. It's crisp, modern and faithful to its roots. I think whatever you decide to do, it's going to be a home run."

My phone rings and breaks the mood. Apologetically, I look up at Aisha. "I'm sorry, I have to take this."

Aisha nods at me and gestures for me to take the call. She pulls her phone out and checks her messages as I answer, "Hello?"

"What in the world do you think you're doing?" I hear Mishka shriek into the phone.

Taking a deep breath, I struggle to remember what Jeff told me so I can answer calmly. "I'm sorry Mishka I can't talk to you. If you want to speak to me, you need to have your lawyer contact my lawyer."

"You moron. You think you can take on the likes of me in court? Bring it on!" Abruptly, the phone goes dead. I breathe a sigh of relief.

When I turn around, I realize Aisha witnessed the whole conversation. Unfortunately, Mishka was shouting, so it's likely Aisha heard both sides. This cannot be happening. Having two clients observe epic, knockdown, drag out fights with Mishka is absolutely unacceptable. My luck couldn't be any worse.

Aisha raises an eyebrow at me. "I take it you all didn't have an amicable separation."

I laugh out loud. "It was anything but. I don't know what happened and I don't know how to fix it."

Aisha picks up a seam ripper from my sewing table. "Wouldn't it be fun if we could take one of these and change everything that isn't going well in our lives?"

"I'm not sure I'd want to change what happened. Because of this, I met Cristiano, and through Cristiano, I met you. If Mishka hadn't gotten on her high horse and criticized me in front of a customer, I might not have felt the need to leave."

"Did she do that often?" Aisha asks softly when I glance over at my phone like it's going to bite me.

"Often enough — especially recently." A horrifying thought occurs to me as I turn to Aisha with wide eyes. "All of this is off the record, right?"

"Of course it is. Today, I'm not a fashion reporter — I'm just a friend. Pretend we're having coffee or something."

"Thanks. I could use a few friends in my corner. All this drama because I left my job? It makes no sense."

"You can't let this woman dismantle everything you've built in your life because she doesn't like you — that's petty and stupid on her part. If you have done nothing wrong, she shouldn't be allowed to destroy your career."

Aisha's phone chimes. She glowers as she examines the message. She walks over to the love seat in the corner and sits down as she exclaims, "Oh, please tell me she didn't just do that —"

"Do what?" I ask steeling myself against the revelation. "Things have been going so well, I don't want to think about all of this blowing up in my face."

"Do you still have Mishka's website on your phone?" Aisha asks reluctantly.

"Yeah, I used to manage it for her."

"Well, you might want to take a look at what she's posted, but, be forewarned — it's not going to be a pleasant experience."

With trepidation, I look up the website I used to know so well. I don't recognize much of anything. There's a video automatically playing. Mishka is berating me for everything I've ever done for her. As I watch, it's like being awake during a nightmare. When my knees start to buckle from the shock of it all, Aisha stands up and guides me to the couch she was sitting on.

"This is horrible! She is not even remotely telling the truth. How do I prove something didn't happen?"

"I don't know. I think it's something your lawyers need to figure out. You have to do something. You can't let her get away with this."

"You sound like Cristiano. He's been telling me the same thing."

"Your boyfriend is not only hunky, he's very smart."

"He was the one who insisted I retain somebody to act as my attorney. Right now, I have a family friend helping me. If it gets any more complicated, I'll have to find someone new. Jeff works for the prosecutor's office now. He doesn't have his own practice."

"There's this one attorney I'm thinking of. She helped a blogger friend of mine defend her work when it was stolen. Unfortunately, she's based in California."

"She can steer me to someone local, I suppose." I sigh as I gather my hair up into a ponytail and tie it with a stray piece of elastic I left on the couch. "I hate that I have to do this. I don't know why she thinks I'm a threat to her."

"Maybe she's jealous of your talent," Aisha suggests. "It happens."

"Cristiano told me as much," I admit. "I'll make some calls on Monday."

"Please do. Enough bad news — let's do something more fun," Aisha says, as she pulls a book of fabric samples on to her lap and starts to flip through the pages.

"That sounds like one of the best ideas I've heard all day."

"That's the spirit. If there's anything I can do, let me know." The sincerity in her voice is humbling. For someone who just met me, she's pretty adamant in her defense of me. It's gratifying for sure — now I need to prove my worth.

"You've gone above and beyond to help promote me. I'll be busy for the next two years just from the short interview you did."

Aisha shrugs. "I didn't do much, I just asked you questions, you took it by the horns and answered them in a way which was honest and forthright. Fans respond to the truth. They don't like fake drama."

"Well, let's not give them any drama. I'm not going to fight this battle over the Internet or in the tabloids. This is too important to leave it up to the court of public opinion."

"I agree. You can't win a spitting war with Mishka. You're going to have to look at the long game."

"Well, here's hoping that the long game doesn't take too long," I reply with a heavy sigh. "I need to get on with my life. I want to be able to make clothes for clients like you. With this shadow hanging over my head, I don't know how I'm going to be able to function."

Aisha moves her hair out of her eyes before she says, "I've learned the hard way that the only way to cope with all the stuff is to do it one day at a time. With skill and talent like yours, you are going to have your own success outside of the drama with her. You just have to wait for it to resolve."

"I feel like I should give you a discount because of all the great advice you've been giving me," I offer.

"Don't you dare. You are trying to build a business. I can afford to pay you. You have no idea what a ridiculous sum of money they pay me to evaluate what people wear — it's crazy. Consider your fee my attempt to pay it forward."

I breathe a sigh of relief. "Thank you so much. I'm going to need the money for an attorney. Mishka needs to pay for trying to destroy me."

⸺ ⬥ ⸺

After Aisha leaves, I pick up my cell phone with shaking hands and call Jeff.

As soon as he answers, I blurt, "I need to launch our plan."

"Are you sure? Winning defamation suits is not an easy task. It's exceptionally hard to prove you didn't do something."

"Hold on, I'm going to send you a link." I walk over to my computer and email Jeff. A minute or so later, I hear Jeff whistle softly. "I get it. I want to make sure I understand this correctly, you never had any joint projects with Mishka, did you?"

"No! I didn't. I always wanted to, but she constantly kept me busy with other stuff. She kept telling me she would promote me to a designer position whenever she thought I was ready. Apparently, she never did."

"As much as I hate to say this, I don't think I'm best suited to help you. However, I went to school with a lawyer who is as sharp as a whip. She works civil litigation, so defamation is right up her alley. Her name is CJ Wells. I'll give her a heads up that I sending you over."

I almost sob in frustration. "Jeff, that probably means I can't do anything. I don't have money to pay an attorney."

"Don't sweat it quite yet. Let me work with CJ and see what we can come up with. She still owes me for helping her pass her Federal Income Tax class. We'll come up with something, I promise. I won't leave you hanging. If there's anything which sets off my fuse, it's people who lie and then bully you into believing it's the truth. I had a stepfather like that once, it's not something I tolerate much. I'll do everything in my power to help you."

Tears are streaming down my face. "I don't even know what to say," I choke out through my tears. "I don't really deserve all of this."

"Of course you do. You are family and this is the kind of thing we do for each other," Jeff explains.

CHAPTER TWELVE

CRISTIANO

JORDAN LOOKS DIFFERENT TONIGHT; She seems a little tired and stressed, but happier and optimistic.

"You're chipper today."

"I met with the attorney Jeff suggested, and she's cool. She seems to think Mishka is on the losing side of the argument. I guess my paranoia that comes from being a little sister of a guy who likes to play practical jokes serves me well," she answers with a self-deprecating smile.

"What do you mean?" I ask, eager to hear the story behind the story.

"When we were younger, Jaxson was always concerned about how casual I was when I posted things on the internet. So, he would routinely break into my accounts and post embarrassing reminders for me all my friends could see. Eventually, I got more savvy about keeping him out of my personal business. He taught me well — because I still do these things now. I kept documentation of everything I posted on Mishka's site and my passwords are locked down tight. I insisted she do the same. Apparently, this obsession is going to save my butt."

"Are you saying there's no way you could've had access to any of Mishka's files without there being a long, complicated paper trail?" I clarify.

"Well, I don't know if it's paper or if it's digital, but that's the gist of it."

"Wouldn't those records belong to Mishka? How do you know she won't destroy or alter them?"

"Well, here's the deal — Mishka didn't want me to impose all these levels of security. To prove a point, I added a backup feature to our computers. Everything accessed on our network was backed up to a third-party provider."

"That's great, but it's still Mishka's data. She can manipulate it any way she wants."

"There's a funny story about that. Mishka never wanted the extra security. She told me if I wished to keep it, I needed to pay for it out of my own pocket."

"What? That's outrageous. It benefits her business, not you personally."

"That's true, but remember I always figured at some point I would be her partner and I would need to have all the business records safe and sound."

"Whoa! It sounds like you made the best move when you quit. She was walking all over you."

Jordan twists her hair in her fingers. The smile slides off her face as she somberly explains, "It's a little too late to have any regrets now. Now, I have to protect my butt.

Since I am the one who pays for the service, I can download a backup of all the data."

My jaw goes slack in surprise as I ask, "You can do all that remotely?"

"I wasn't considered an administrative assistant extraordinaire for nothing," Jordan declares smugly. "I know her office inside and out. We were on the road at fashion shows a bunch so, I needed to be able to get work done when we were away from the office, so I set up the computers so we would both have access to our files from anywhere, even overseas."

I feel my eyes widen in surprise when the implication her words hits me. Not quite able to hide my shock I ask, "You're going to lock her out of her own work? That seems like a really risky strategy."

"That's the beauty of what I'm going to do, I'm going to get a full backup of the system and give it to my attorney to do whatever magic they do to determine which dates files were created or deleted and who had access to what, when. The bottom line is after this is done, it's all in the hands of CJ. I don't have to have sleepless nights over it anymore. Somebody more qualified than I am is taking care of it. Even though I'm still worried about what Mishka can do to me, it's a huge weight off my shoulders."

"I'm proud of you for hanging tough against all this controversy. I know it's hard and I'm confident you did nothing she's accusing you of. You are not responsible for what's happening to you. We should celebrate this like a victory," I declare with a wicked smile. "That always calls for a party."

Jordan looks into the camera. "There's only one problem with that — or did you forget you're in another state?"

I slump in my chair. "Sadly, I can't forget. How about we go on a virtual date?"

"A virtual date?" Jordan asks.

"One of my friends was in a long-distance relationship. He and his girlfriend would do things like eat the same foods at the same time so it seemed like they were having dinner together and they would watch the same movie while on the phone with each other. They could comment and talk as if they were on a real date."

"I have a question."

"Shoot," I reply as I adjust my camera on the computer.

"Are we actually dating?"

"If I lived in town with you, we would be dating. I won't lie. It sucks not being able to be with you. I enjoy your company and you make me smile. So, this feels awkward and strange, but I would rather have this than no contact with you at all."

"Me too. I guess this makes us official."

I grin like a fool. "Official it is. Since we've cleared all that up, do you want to choose a movie from Netflix we can watch together?"

"I'll leave it up to you. I'll choose the snack foods. I make better snacking choices than you do."

"Hey, it wasn't my fault the only chips I had in the house when you came were jalapeño. I didn't know Jubilee took the rest of them for a party at her house.

Usually, I stock my pantry better."

Jordan sticks her tongue out at me. "That might be true, but I still get to choose the snack foods."

I give Jordan a puzzled look. "Wouldn't it be easier for you to choose the movie and for me to choose my own snack foods?"

Jordan shrugs. "Perhaps, but it's more of a challenge this way. Besides, I might've added some food items the last time I was there."

I walk away from the camera and yell back toward my desk, "Just a second I need to take inventory, I'll be right back."

I open my freezer and notice a bunch of food I didn't even know was in there. I grab a couple before I rush back to the camera and announce, "You are officially my hero. I love Häagen-Dazs ice cream bars. How did you know that?"

"I didn't. I love them too," she responds a shy smile. "I guess it means we're compatible."

I rub my chin thoughtfully as I tease, "It might be a little early to tell. I think we need to list our favorite movies first."

<hr>

When I yawn again, Rowden signals to the cameraman to cut. "What is with you today? We actually have to film this segment without you yawning all the way through it."

"I know, I'm just exhausted."

Rowden wiggles his eyebrows suggestively. "Girlfriend keeping you up all night?"

I level my gaze at him. "In a weird way, I guess I do."

Rowden dramatically cringes. "Do I even want to know what you're talking about?"

"Oh shut up!" I rub my tired eyes. "You don't know what you're talking about."

"So, why don't you tell me? 'Cause I have no idea."

"Remember Jordan Shepherd?"

"Yeah, she was the designer chick you ended up with after you fired the one I wanted you to use."

"Well, I'm glad I fired Mishka. Jordan is absolutely brilliant. It turns out we click. We click a lot. She is bright and surprisingly snarky."

"Sounds like the perfect match for you."

"I think so too, but it's hard to date when we live in completely different time zones."

"I suppose you'll abandon our show and move," Rowden says with a sour look.

I wave Rowden's concerns away. "We're still getting to know each other."

"You might not put enough effort into our show now that you're distracted by some chick."

"I've known Jordan for several months now, this is the first time I've had an issue. It seems you came into the studio the other day not feeling so great either," I challenge.

"Yeah, well that's different because I'm your boss, and Jubilee and I were celebrating."

"I might argue with the assessment that you're my

boss. When we started everything together, we were equal partners; you happen to do the executive director duties. Without me, it would be difficult to do the show," I argue as my frustration grows.

"Don't be one of those guys who suddenly makes stupid decisions over some hot young thing in a tight skirt."

Rowden's offhand remark stings a little. I thought after all these years, he would trust me. I've gotten my crap together and I can adult with the best of them.

My anger is starting to build as I swivel my chair around and scowl at him. "I don't always make boneheaded decisions," I respond in a voice sharper than I intend. I roll my bad shoulder and try to massage a muscle cramp out before adding, "Oh, by the way, we seriously have to change the name of the show."

"Jubilee doesn't want to change the name."

"That's funny — because when I spoke to her, she said she thought it would be a good idea."

Rowden looks surprised. "She loves that word."

I lean forward in my chair. "She never intended for you to name the show *Xyresic.*"

"You're wrong. If we're going to start talking about changes, I think we should cover fewer races directly and focus more on the private lives of the athletes. You know, the kind of stuff in the tabloids. People eat that stuff up. I mean, look how well TMZ and E! are doing."

I stand up quickly and flinch when my knee starts to buckle. "You couldn't be more wrong. We're not some gossip rag. We inform people about the X-Games and focus on motocross and BMX. We serve a special market and have lots of dedicated fans. If we go changing the show to something unrecognizable, we'll lose viewership."

"All I know is everywhere I turn, people like the Kardashians are all over. We need a family like that in racing to attract an audience."

I rub my temples as I say, "Today we'll have to agree to disagree. I can't even wrap my brain around what you're proposing. I have a colossal headache, and I feel like I'm going to upchuck any second. I'm going to go home."

"What about the show?" Rowden asks desperately.

"I don't know," I snap as I sway just a bit. "Maybe you should interview some celebrity or something."

"What in the world is going on? You never miss a show."

"I guess today I'm going to, because if I don't get home I'll pass out right here in the studio."

"I'll call Jubilee and have her give you a ride home." Rowden studies me anxiously. "I hope you don't have the flu. If you do, our show is screwed this week."

"Give Zane a call, he's been champing at the bit to get on the air." I slump back in my chair and try to cover my eyes.

"That's not a bad idea; the kid is pretty good. Go home and get well. I don't want you to bring your germs to work and get us all sick. Jubs and I are planning a cruise."

Jubilee comes flying through the door. "Rowden!

Don't be a jerk." She turns to me. "Come on. I'm going to take you home. You look like you're about to collapse."

"I'll try not to," I answer in a shaky voice, but privately, I wonder if I can even make it to the car.

<hr>

I struggle to roll over and grab my phone. When I finally get it, I accidentally push the button to accept a video call. I must look really awful because when Jordan sees me, she exclaims, "What happened to you?"

I shift positions, prop a pillow behind me, and move the ice pack to a different spot on my neck. I run my hand through my unruly hair. "I don't know Jor. I feel awful. I was at work, and it hit all of a sudden."

Jordan springs up from her couch. "I'll be right back."

I'm a little startled by her abrupt departure. I reach down beside the bed and grab my bottle of water as I waited for her to come back. Even bending down makes me dizzy.

When I pick up my phone again, it's Jaxson on the other end instead of Jordan. It's a little jarring. I must not have hidden my expression well. Jaxson gives me a crooked grin as he says, "I know I'm not as pretty as my sister, but she thought I might be able to help you. What's up with you?"

"I wish I knew. I was at work today and got clobbered with a colossal headache. I feel like my guts are being turned inside out too." I use a wet washcloth to wipe the sweat from my forehead.

Jaxson pulls a little notepad from his pocket and begins to write notes. "Do you get headaches a lot?"

I nod carefully as I say, "Yeah, I've had migraines since I was a kid, but they've been under control for a while. Usually, I have some warning."

"Is this headache worse than your migraines?" Jaxson asks with a frown.

"No, I don't think so."

"Well, I usually do shoulders and knees. General Practice is a little out of my league. I haven't worked in that specialty since I was a resident."

"Someday, I'll have to talk to you about your specialty. I don't think I can handle telling you about all the ways my body is screwed today. I did a number on it during my racing career."

"I understand," Jaxson says with a sympathetic smile. "We human beings are often hard on our bodies. You wouldn't believe the stories I hear in my line of work."

"So, what do you think is wrong with me?" I ask as another wave of nausea hits.

"I think you probably have a bad migraine or maybe a virus of some sort. You just need to lay low and make sure you drink lots of fluids. If you're not feeling better in the morning, go to the doctor and get some medications and have them put you on an IV drip, so you don't get dehydrated."

"Okay, Doc. I'll do my best," I respond weakly.

"I was serious about the other stuff too; there have been some remarkable advances in joint repair. Jordan tells me you have quite a bit of shoulder pain. We should talk about your options. You shouldn't have to live in so much pain."

I sigh as I move the icepack from my neck to my forehead. "I wish I felt well enough to celebrate the news."

Jaxson laughs as he says, "You need to rest. When you feel better, we should talk. I'll catch you later."

Jordan's face appears on my phone. "Did my big brother fix you all up?"

"There's not much he can do to help me today, but he might be able to fix me up in the future."

"I am relieved to hear it. Take care of yourself, and I'll call back later to check in on you, okay?"

"Yeah, but I can't guarantee I'll answer my phone. I am feeling pretty exhausted. — I don't want you to freak out."

"I'll try not to worry, but I can't guarantee I'll be successful." Jordan teases as she blows me a kiss.

"Well, at least try because I don't want you to ruin your design mojo by stressing out about me." I retort.

"Sorry to tell you, Cristiano, I worry about you whether you're here or there … healthy or sick. Get some sleep. I'll be thinking of you." She blows a kiss at me before she hangs up the phone.

Even though I feel like something the cat dragged in, I still grin from ear to ear. It sure is nice to have somebody in my life who gives a care. This feeling could become downright addictive.

Chapter Thirteen

Jordan

"I CAN'T BELIEVE YOU flew all the way here to be with me on Labor Day weekend," I exclaim as I pick up Cristiano at the airport. "This is becoming a pretty regular trip for me. Our relationship is going to make you broke." I thread my fingers through his long thick hair and pull him down for a deep, leisurely kiss.

Cristiano shoots me a grin as he grabs his suitcase. "I got lucky this time; they had a big sale on airfare, and I snagged tickets a while ago before I got sick. It would've been a shame for me to let the ticket go to waste; it was nonrefundable."

"You're a little crazy, you know that? I don't know very many people who would fly through a couple states to hang out with me for a weekend."

He places his arm around my waist as he jokes, "Maybe I didn't just come to see you. Perhaps I came to thank your brother for all his help."

"That would earn you extra brownie points. I like guys with impeccable manners. Just let me know when

135

you want to lavish the praise on."

"We could take Donda and Jaxson out to dinner or something."

I grab Cristiano's hand as we walk through the airport concourse pulling his carry-on bag behind him. "Sounds fun. I don't think I've ever been on a double date with my brother."

"How are your projects going?" Cristiano asks me.

"Actually, it's a good thing you showed up in person — having you here makes it easier to make last-minute adjustments to the jackets I created for you. Originally, I planned to make you two, but then I found this gorgeous fabric which will look spectacular in front of the camera."

Cristiano squeezes my hand. "You don't have to keep making me clothes. I know you're trying to build up a broad, diverse portfolio. If it's full of jackets sized for me, I'm not sure how helpful it will be."

"Don't worry about it," I reply with an excited grin. "You wouldn't believe all the stuff I've been creating recently. It's been so much fun. I guess I never realized exactly how many people need help to find clothes."

Cristiano stops in front of a restaurant in the airport. "I don't know about you, but I'm starving. Why don't we stop and get a bite to eat and you can tell me what you've been up to?"

After the waitress takes our order, I continue where I left off. "Well, I've done two things for new clients with disabilities. Aisha has been referring people to JS Couture left and right. One of my favorite new clients is Aisha's grandmother who has terrible arthritis. It turns out Nina would like to dress as fashionably as her granddaughter, but she can't manage the buttons anymore. She hates wearing muumuus and elastic pants. I was able to design fashionable clothes for her with some special magnetic closures. By looking at them, you can't tell they are adaptive pieces. Nina is so excited that it's a blast to create new designs for her with clever fasteners which she can manage with her arthritis."

Cristiano shows me his wrist. "I've busted this thing more than once. The first time I broke it, I was shocked I couldn't even do simple things like buttoning my jeans. Your clothing could be a godsend."

"Thank you, it's really gratifying to use all my education to help other people. My next customer was even more challenging than you."

"Why? Was she as clueless about fashion as I am?" Cristiano asks.

"No, Laura is quite knowledgeable about fashion, but unfortunately she could never make any of it work for her. She has a severe spine deformity which makes her hunchbacked and makes her limbs look like they are different lengths. All Laura wanted was to be the maid of honor in her sister's wedding, but they couldn't find anything off the rack to fit. They were both so disappointed — but Aisha told her to come to me."

"I am sensing a theme here. Aisha seems like a walking billboard for you," Cristiano replies as he pops a French fry in his mouth. "I take it you were able to work around Laura's issues?"

"It took several tries and different kinds of patterns, but eventually, I was able to design a dress which flatters Laura. The bonus is style-wise it matches with the rest of the bridesmaids. For once, Laura felt like she fit in. They sent me pictures the other day of the wedding, and she looked gorgeous. I have never been prouder of myself."

"So, this could be a viable career path for you, huh?"

I press my lips together in a thin line as I share my frustration. "Well, there is a downside. In New York, Mishka had a ridiculously large clientele made up of stars. She even designed costumes for Broadway. Those folks can afford to pay quite well. Mishka could reinvest in fabrics and new design techniques. Unfortunately, the clients I've been helping are often struggling themselves. Not everyone is independently wealthy like you," I add with a smile.

"I don't know the answer. It seems to me like the services you are providing are more than needed. Maybe, you could get a grant or something to cover the cost of designing for people who couldn't otherwise afford custom clothes."

"What a great idea!" I exclaim as I give Cristiano a grateful smile. "I don't want to have to stop doing what I'm doing, but I'd also like to eat and find a place of my own. If I keep taking on clients who are as broke as I am, I'm never going to get ahead."

"Sometimes, building up good karma is better than a fancy meal."

"Sadly, I can't eat good karma, and I don't want to keep mooching off of my brother. I'm a little too grown-up to be pulling that kind of stunt."

"I see your point, but there has to be a happy medium somewhere. I'm sorry it's turning out to be a big struggle."

"I have to admit I miss my New York-sized paycheck, but I feel better about myself when I look in the mirror." I heave a sigh and try to shake off my funky mood. "I'll figure it out somehow. I always do."

———⬤●⬤———

My brother gives Cristiano an apologetic look. "I'm sorry about your shoulder, I didn't even think about it when we chose bowling for our date."

"No, it's all right. It's been a while since I've had an opportunity to compete at anything. So, even though my body is killing me, it's been fun."

I raise my eyebrow at Cristiano. "If that's the way you play injured, I'd hate to see how well you do when you're feeling one hundred percent. You wiped the floor with all of us. Even though I used to be an athlete, I can't keep up with you."

Cristiano comes over and gives me a brief, but thorough kiss. "Next time, I might even let you win."

I reach up and grab him by the shirt as I pull him close for a kiss. "Who says I'm not winning now?" I answer with a wink. Breaking away from Cristiano, I glance over at Donda. "I'm starving, I'm going to go grab a hot dog or something. You guys want to join us?"

Donda catches Jaxson's eye. "Nah, go ahead. I'm going to demand a rematch for the last game. I've got something to prove to my husband."

The competitive gleam in Donda's eyes is intense. I walk over to my brother and pat him on the shoulder. "I wish you good luck, Jax. I think your wife intends to bury you in utter brilliance."

Jaxson studies his wife with appreciation before he says, "She does that every single day. All I can hope for is that she consoles the loser."

Before Cristiano and I can gather up our gear to go to the little restaurant in the bowling alley, his phone rings.

Cristiano grimaces. "I'm sorry, I have to take this."

Cristiano turns to head toward the door because the noise level in the bowling alley is deafening. As I move to sit back down in the hard, plastic chairs, Cristiano grabs my hand. "Come keep me company."

Waving goodbye to my family, I get up to follow him. "It's a bit stuffy in here, I could use some fresh air."

As soon as we get out into the parking lot, Cristiano answers the call that's been coming in every thirty seconds. Cristiano tucks me against his chest as the wind starts to blow.

I feel Cristiano's body fill with tension as he listens. I don't know who is on the other phone, but whoever they are they are more than pissed off. I can hear him yelling at Cristiano even though the phone is not up to my ear.

"You didn't tell me you added a production meeting on the schedule. The last word I had from you guys was to 'have a good holiday'," Cristiano counters after listening for a few seconds. "As far as I know, the next time I'm due at the studio is Wednesday."

Cristiano listens for a few moments and says, "Relax, Rowden. I've got my computer with me and I'm reviewing footage. It's not as if I completely abandoned the show. I'm on vacation like a lot of other people this weekend."

Rowden must be even more agitated because he is speaking loudly enough I can almost make out every syllable.

Cristiano pulls the phone away from his ear. After a couple of moments, he puts it back. "What do you mean the new direction of the show?" he asks with a look of dread. He scrubs his hand down his face. "I told you I thought it was a bad idea … yes, I know that you are executive director — but, I co-created this with you. I should have a say in the future of our show."

I can clearly hear the guy shout, "It's my call. Take it or leave it." Abruptly, the phone goes dead. Cristiano is holding his cell phone in midair as if he's lost.

"Are you all right?" I whisper softly as I turn around in his arms and give him a hug.

"He's trying to change everything which makes our show unique."

I pivot in his arms so I'm facing him and start to rub the knots out of his neck. My brain goes into high gear as I try to figure out how to help him. "What does your contract say?" I lower my voice. "Is there an out if the two of you have creative differences?"

Cristiano heaves out a breath as if it's painful. "I don't know. I signed something, but it was so long ago I don't remember what it said." He reaches up and grabs his shoulder. "Maybe bowling was not such a great idea."

"I can get you some ice from the little deli —"

Cristiano shakes his head, and he pulls me closer. "Maybe later. I suppose I should probably dig out my contract and study it again. If Rowden doesn't come to his senses soon, I'm not sure I even want to be part of the show anymore."

"If there isn't a non-compete agreement, maybe you don't have to be. You could pursue a show with your own vision. You have your own social media following, and the fans would probably come with you. After all, you are the face of the show, your business partner isn't."

"This sucks because Rowden and Jubilee have been my friends for years. I don't want to abandon all the work we've put into our show. That would be a little crazy. Starting from scratch is crazy difficult. Look at Oprah Winfrey and her network. Even with as much name recognition as Oprah has, she still struggles with programming."

"It's a tough situation all around, but if you guys can't work it out, it might be worth thinking about."

Cristiano pulls me closer. "You know, the thing I hate about this most is that Rowden intruded on my magical weekend with you. Now, my brain is going to be busy turning over ideas in my head about how to deal with all this crap."

Standing on my tiptoes, I thread my arms around Cristiano's neck and kiss him passionately. I break the kiss and try to catch my breath. The man kisses so well my knees shake. "I guess I'll have to do my best to distract you. It's not likely you'll be able to do anything about it all this weekend anyway. We might as well take advantage of your break."

"That sounds like a great plan. Still, I'm not sure what I'm going to do if Rowden is serious about take it or leave it." Cristiano slumps against the building and puts his chin on the top of my head as he holds me in a loose embrace.

CHAPTER FOURTEEN

CRISTIANO

THE FLIGHT BACK TO Aspen seems to go in slow motion and light speed at the same time. Saying goodbye to Jordan is more difficult every time I see her. Long distance relationships are a pain in the neck — sometimes literally. I adjust the little travel pillow Jordan made me as I try to make myself comfortable.

Jordan was true to her word when she said she would be my biggest distraction. In massive road trip we traveled across the state of Oregon to visit the Painted Hills. Jordan was thrilled when I found her a handcrafted sewing box at an outdoor arts and craft market along the way.

On Labor Day, she treated me to an Aidan O'Brien concert. I guess there are perks to being friends with the musician's wife. It was pretty radical to hang out with Aidan and his band after the concert. Back in the day, when I was a well-known athlete, people clamored for my attention. However, I get the sense everyone in this group are close friends and don't really care about Aidan's star status.

That's the kind of relationship I want to replicate on our show. I want people to be able to know we'll treat them like regular human beings with real emotions and feelings. I want them to be honest and open in interviews without always anticipating a secret gotcha question which may put them in the tabloid news. I just want people to understand the world of competition that is part of the X-Games. I have no interest in dragging people through the gutter.

Rowden has turned our show into something I never meant it to be. Now, a showdown with him is inevitable. I have a hunch I'll come out the loser. Whenever we have discussions about our show, Jubilee usually sides with Rowden. He'll value her opinion more than mine — I can almost guarantee it. I'm torn about this meeting with Rowden. Part of me is dreading it, but the other part of me wants to get it over with. At least if I can sort out what's going on with *Xyresic*, I'll know how to make plans for the future. Right now, I am in limbo.

I study the statistics I compiled from our show and other shows like it. If I'm going to go into battle for my professional life, I need to be prepared.

⸺•⸺

Rowden watches me come in the room. "Well, if your bum knee has anything to say about your weekend, you and the girlfriend were more than a little busy."

I flinch. "I don't see how it's any of your business. What I do on my own time is up to me."

"If it affects your performance, it is my business.

You missed a critically important meeting. Don't you care about our show any more?"

"You can't blame me for missing a meeting I didn't know about. Did you put it on anyone's schedule? Did you send an email out about it? Did you give me a phone call?"

"Uh, no," Rowden concedes. "I told one of the media interns to tell you about it."

I look at the calendar on my phone. "Nope. I got nothing."

"You probably wouldn't have liked what happened in the meeting anyway. Your absence may have been for the best."

"Do I even want to know what happened?" I ask with trepidation. "You don't usually do stuff like this. What happened to making decisions together? I thought we were partners."

Rowden shrugs. "You didn't care enough about *Xyresic* to be here for the meeting, so we voted to revamp the entire show. People are interested in athletes as commodities now, not for straightforward athletic prowess," Rowden answers calmly, as if he wasn't dropping a bombshell that could destroy the future of *Xyresic*.

"Wow. Who is 'we'? We used to be us — back when we acted like partners. I have some stats here which show —"

"Just think about it. Most of the country didn't even know who that football player, Tom Brady, was until his cheating controversy. Since the tabloids and the entertainment media started digging into his personal life, he has become more popular than ever."

I drag my hand through my hair. "I don't think popularity on TMZ has anything to do with how well we meet the needs of our fan base."

Rowden draws himself up to his full height. "Well, Jubilee thinks is a solid move."

"If we are comparing the advice of our significant others, Jordan thinks it's a terrible idea," I argue.

"If you're going to be more loyal to your girlfriend than to Jubilee and I, after all we built together, we need to reconsider our relationship with you too," Rowden threatens as he storms out of the room.

———◆———

As soon as Jordan's video camera clicks on, she gasps. "Oh, no! Your meeting didn't go very well, did it?"

I take a long drink of my beer before I answer. "No, it didn't. Basically, everything I hoped wouldn't happen, did. I don't know what's going on with Rowden. I couldn't convince him that if he changes the show so radically, we are going to lose more fans than we gain. It's like he's completely lost the vision we started out with. I don't understand."

"Does Rowden usually make emotional decisions?" Jordan asks.

"No!" I blurt as I try to fit all the pieces of the puzzle together. Since the meeting ended, I have done little else. "That's the thing; I'm usually the spontaneous one, Rowden is the guy who does detailed market research."

"Do you suppose he did?" Jordan asks as she adjusts her halter top.

Her graceful movements are mesmerizing. I can't tear my eyes away. I would give anything to be in her arms tonight.

"Do what?" I ask fighting the distraction caused by the sight of Jordan's body. "By the way, I love the new shirt. Is that the fabric we picked out at the craft market?"

"Yeah, it is so hot. I decided to make myself a new summer shirt even though out of season. I thought the scrap of material would be cute. I definitely don't need the quilt I was going to make, right now. Although, I think I have enough fabric left over to make both."

"Well, you look fantastic. I wish I was there. I would love to be the one tying your shirt — or untying it. If I was there, I would kiss every inch of your skin. You are so beautiful."

Jordan flushes to a dusky shade of rose. "Thank you, I'm still getting used to not wearing body makeup."

"I noticed you stopped. Is it working out okay for you?"

"I decided if my clients could cope with people staring at them, who am I to complain about uneven skin tone? Basically, they gave me the courage to be honest about what I really look like. Surprisingly, it hasn't been as big an issue as I remember it being when I was a teenager."

I pull my shirt aside and show her the Hurricane on my chest. "I got this years ago when I won enough from one race to pay for a new bike. It was a huge deal back then, but no one blinks over tats or piercings now. Maybe people are more flexible about what they consider 'normal'."

Jordan nods. "I think you're probably right. There seems to be a lot more acceptance in general. I saw the trend in the fashion industry too. When I first started, models looked like clones of each other. But by the time I left Mishka Unlimited, people of different sizes, shapes, and ages were being featured at Fashion Week and in other big name shows. That's a good thing for people who look like me."

"You mean other stunning women with beautiful eyes and gorgeous hair?" I ask.

Jordan makes a funny face at me. "You're so sweet. That's not what I meant. I was referring to being black."

"Maybe it's because I am biracial, but I see only your gorgeousness."

Jordan pauses and then seems to choose her words carefully. "Unfortunately, not everyone sees the world through your eyes. This may sound disrespectful, but I don't mean it to be. Do you think race is playing any part in Rowden's decision to move the show away from what you would like it to be?"

Her words stop me in my tracks. Even as I ponder the idea, I dismiss it. I can't even fathom Rowden and Jubilee consciously discriminating against me. "We built the show together. If he has issues with my race, he should've said something long before now."

She shrugs. "I've had racism show up in many different ways. Sometimes, the most dangerous people are not the ones who say they hate you based on your race. It's the ones who swear up and down they don't see color because they have X amount of friends who are black, Hispanic, Asian or whatever — but then behind your back, they complain about 'people like you'."

"Isn't that the truth? When I was in high school, I used to deliver pizzas and my supervisor would always give me the delivery van which was prone to breaking down. One day I asked him why I always got the worst van even though I had the most seniority. He just looked at me and said, 'People like you aren't used to driving any better'."

Jordan's jaw drops. "Wow! Just wow. I don't have anything to say."

"That's okay. My dad ended up getting the last laugh when my boss had to go through him to get a zoning variance for his business. The idiot didn't even know my father was the mayor of our town."

"That's spectacular," Jordan exclaims with a laugh. "'There is no revenge quite as good as being successful, right?'"

"My dad thought it was quite satisfactory too," I comment with a chuckle as I recall my dad telling the story with lots of animation. "I don't know what's behind his decisions. I can't imagine that my race plays any kind of role. Rowden is always the one to make really logical decisions. This time, his whole rationale seems to be reality TV shows do well on cable."

"What are you going to do about it?"

I rub my shoulder. "I don't know. If we have to part ways, it'd be a huge disappointment. We've been friends for so long. I don't know why we can't work this out. It's hard. Every time before, we've been able to talk through our differences, but this time, I can't seem to get through to him. He's not listening to me."

"Could you start over again if you had to?" Jordan pulls her hair up off her neck and fans herself.

I think about her question for a few moments. "I suppose I could. It would mean starting over again from scratch. Rowden and I built this show out of a podcast I could go back to those roots and build up another fan base."

Jordan frowns. "I hate to think of you and I both in the same spot of needing to reinvent ourselves to be successful, but it looks like that might be what needs to happen. It's a scary place to be."

"True. It is, but part of me can't help but celebrate the upside of this. If I could start over again, I could be anywhere. Lord knows I fly all over creation anyway — if Rowden and I part ways and take different paths, there's no reason I couldn't be based out of Oregon."

Jordan sighs. "Now you've put me in an awful jam. I don't know if I should root for you to keep your job and work things out because it would make you happy or if I should root for you completely losing your job so we can be close together. It's a terrible dilemma."

I snicker at Jordan. "This is my career we're talking about, and I'm not sure which option I want either. Since my career is all up in the air, let's talk about yours. Do you have any great news? I could use a distraction."

Suddenly, Brando starts barking frantically. Through the eyes of the camera and from several states away, I can't tell what's going on. When Jordan stops laughing, I ask, "What was that all about?"

"I keep telling that silly puppy to leave my hair bands alone — but Brando won't listen. He's managed to twist it around his back leg. Apparently, he thinks it's viciously attacking him. So, he's trying to get untangled and complain at the same time. He's frustrated because he keeps falling over."

"Oh, poor guy. I miss him."

"He's a tough little dude. Unfortunately, he's also an incredibly huge pest. Getting any sewing done around him is quite a challenge. He likes to attack my material as I feed it through the serger. That's one of the reasons Jaxson talked about getting a commercial space. He thinks I should open a boutique. I don't know if he actually believes in my vision or if he just wants me out of his house. I'm trying to keep a low profile and not bother them — but you never know."

"I think it sounds like a great idea for you to open a boutique. You've already identified an under-served market. You could become a specialty shop without much trouble. It would be a cinch to write up a business plan for you."

"I would go for it in a heartbeat, but I don't want to take advantage of my brother."

"Having met your brother, I don't think he would offer to do something he wasn't genuinely supportive of. I don't believe this move has anything to do with whether you leave wet towels on the floor in the bathroom or don't set the table the same way they do. Your brother strikes me as the kind of guy who would tell you if you were doing something which bothered him."

Jordan looks away from the camera and looks sad for a moment. "You're probably right. Whenever Jaxson has an issue with what I do, he usually finds a way to tell me about it."

"Exactly! Obviously, if your brother wants to help you start a boutique, it's because he believes in your dream."

"It's true. He's always been one of my biggest fans, regardless of what path I choose to take."

I lean forward and look directly in the web camera before I say, "I think it would be a great idea for you to explore this route with him. What harm could it do?"

"I still have the legal thing with Mishka hanging over my head." I can tell she's upset because she's chewing on her bottom lip. After a couple of seconds, she admits, "I hate to make any permanent moves involving my future until I know what's happening with my past."

"Hopefully, it will be resolved soon. I think you should at least look into it to see what you need to do. I have no doubt that when you go into business, it'll take off like a rocket. There are so many people like me who don't fit into regular clothes you'll have an automatic audience."

Jordan twirls a pen in her hand as she lets my words absorb. With a somewhat lopsided smile, she remarks, "Look at us. Both of our lives are a complete mess. So, what are we doing with each other?"

"Making each other happy?" It comes off as a

lighthearted joke, but I haven't been this content in years. I wake up thinking about Jordan, and I go to sleep wondering if she's doing the same. She occupies every empty spot in my soul.

"True enough. You do make me extremely happy. What doesn't thrill me is the fact that you are so far away from me. We have to figure out how to plan our lives better so we don't need to be apart."

"I totally agree. This distance thing royally sucks." I lean back in my computer chair and scrub my hand over my face.

I need to work on getting my life in order so I can start one for real with Jordan. As fun as it has been to have our nightly calls, there is no substitution for holding my girlfriend in my arms.

CHAPTER FIFTEEN

JORDAN

"When is your hunky guy coming back to see you?" Donda asks as she helps me fold a long piece of fabric.

"Oh shoot! What time is it?" I exclaim.

Donda's shrugs. "I don't know — twelve thirty-ish?"

I look down at my ratty cutoffs and tank top in dismay. "I need to get ready. Cristiano is going to be here soon." How did I lose track of time? I thought I set an alarm.

"You're not making your usual journey to PDX?"

"No, he has a car this time. He is interviewing some guy who lives in Grants Pass. Then, he's going to spend the night here and go to Bend to interview a couple members of the extreme skateboarding team."

"Well, it's not a vacation or anything, but at least

you'll be able to spend some time with him. You should go to Bend. You guys could hang out when he's not working."

"Cristiano suggested the same thing — but I was afraid I'd get in the way."

"That's silly. If he invited you, you should go. There are lots of great places to go in Bend."

Without warning, Donda sways and nearly falls down. I help her over to the couch.

"Are you all right?"

Donda's shakes her head slightly. "I don't know. I've been so tired recently, and I'm sweating like a pig. Maybe I got some weird virus or something."

"Your husband is a doctor. Ask him. Actually, never mind … I'll send Jaxson a text message myself. You look awful."

The corner of Donda's mouth hitches up. "Gee, thanks for the reminder. Why would I want my husband to see me when I look awful?" Donda slumps back against the cushions on the couch as she asks, "Would you get me a blanket? I'm feeling a little cold."

My eyebrows fly up as I say, "Wow! You must really be sick. It's not cold in this house. I'll grab you a quilt off my bed."

By the time I get back, my brother is coming through the front door. He is almost sprinting. "Wow, that was fast," I say in surprise as I gently cover Donda with my favorite quilt.

"I was just around the corner," he answers me before he turns to Donda. "What's wrong?"

"A few minutes ago, I got so woozy I couldn't stand. I don't know what's wrong with me. I have been so tired recently, and it's like I'm struggling to breathe. I cough a lot, but I don't really have a cold."

"Just a minute, I'll grab my medical bag," he says as he sprints out of the room. Jaxson comes back and starts to examine Donda. The concern is evident on his face no matter how much he tries to hide it.

I feel awkward just standing there, I don't know if Donda wants me here or if I should discreetly duck out and go hang out in my room. Jaxson's exam seems private and intimate.

Jaxson frowns as he listens to my sister-in-law's chest. He looks up at me as he says, "Can you turn off your fans for a minute? I want to make sure I'm not getting feedback in my stethoscope."

I spring up from the chair I was sitting on and go turn off every fan in the room. Unfortunately, Jaxson's expression doesn't get any better. When he examines her hands, he blows out a deep breath. "Donda, why didn't you say something before? I need to take off your shoes," he instructs as he gently pulls her tennis shoes off. After he examines her toes, he scowls. "We have to find a sitter. I need to take you to the hospital. Where is Gabriel?"

"He's in the middle of a basketball scrimmage. I'm not even sure exactly where he's at. He rode with Ryan Scott," Donda answers as panic starts to edge in. "The neighbor lady who usually babysits for us is out of town."

"I can watch Kennadie. It's not a problem. Why do you have to take Donda to the hospital?" I get Donda's purse off the sideboard. "I'll put your Kindle in here. You might be at the hospital for a while."

"I may be overreacting because I'm not a cardiologist, but I hear a murmur and Donda has a rash on the bottom of her feet. It can be a symptom of endocarditis. I want to get her checked out."

"Sounds pretty scary." I feel a bit breathless from a sudden surge of fear.

"It certainly can be. I need to get her to the ER as soon as I can. Do you have everything handled here?"

"I can handle it. Kennadie is down for a nap right now, so stop worrying. I used to be a nanny — I can manage one by myself."

"Okay, I'll keep you updated. Just let Gabriel know what's going on when he comes home."

***

I'm concentrating so much on the rhythm of the sewing machine that I jump when I get a text message from Cristiano. I smile when I read his request for me to call him. Apparently, he stopped to stretch his legs on the way here. I worry about him; his shoulder and knee seem to be bothering him all the time now.

I decide to surprise him with a video call. "Hey, you! Are you almost here? There's been a slight change of plans. I may still be babysitting when you arrive."

"That sounds fun. I could use a few of Kennadie's giggles. It's been a long day."

"Donda isn't feeling well, so Jaxson is taking her to the ER. It could be a few hours."

Cristiano's brows furrow as he comments, "When

the doc in the family takes you to the ER, it's never a good sign."

"Don't remind me, I'm sewing like a fiend to relieve my stress. You know Jaxson, he doesn't sound the alarm very easily. He's generally downright chill. When I saw the look of terror on his face, it was hard not to freak out right there in front of Donda. I know Jaxson. Whatever is going on is some sort of big deal."

"Is Gabriel around? How is he taking the news?"

"No, he's not here. It'll just be us. Gabriel's at a basketball scrimmage somewhere. I'm not sure when he'll be home."

"Okay, I'll pick up some food for us. Do you want stuff from the Thai place?"

"That sounds good. Kennadie likes their coconut rice. I'll see you in a few minutes. Drive safe."

<hr>

"Any word from your brother yet?" Cristiano asks as he juggles Kennadie and shifts her to his other hip. She is fascinated with his hair and keeps trying to pull it out.

I put my arms out and offer to hold her. At first, she pretends she's going to come to me, but then she tucks herself into Cristiano's chest and won't let go of his shirt. I take my phone out and check it one more time before I answer, "No, the last update I got from him was that they were taking Donda in for evaluation by the ER docs, but he hadn't heard the results of any testing. They were waiting around to hear what the doctor says. I'm a little worried because it's been a couple of hours since I've heard anything from Jaxson. I hope it means he's in a dead zone and Donda hasn't taken a turn for the worse."

"The hospital probably got busy." Cristiano shifts my niece to his other hip. As he does so, he shakes out his shoulder. "For such a little thing, she gets heavy quickly."

I glance at him skeptically. "Or, somebody I know needs to get some work done on his shoulder. Did you ever finish your conversation with my brother about getting it repaired?"

"We've talked a bit, but I haven't had a chance to follow up with him," he answers with a shrug.

"I think you should do something. In the months we've known each other, it has gotten dramatically worse. I saw you grimace at dinner when you were lifting your fork. In case you've forgotten, that's not the usual state of things. You should be able to move without pain."

"I can't remember the last time I was completely without pain. I'm not sure it's even possible."

"Seriously, I think it's getting worse. Do me a favor and have a conversation with Jaxson. He won't lie to you. If he says something can be done, he knows what he's talking about. Jaxson is good about not recommending surgery unless he thinks he can help someone."

"I don't doubt your brother's capabilities. With everything so up in the air about my job, I don't know when I could squeeze a surgery and rehab into my life."

"I'll tell you what Jaxson told me before he recommended my knee surgery. I had been nursing an injury since I played basketball in high school. Jaxson told me the chronic inflammation can do long-term damage too. So, he had one of his colleagues fix it. I don't have nearly as much trouble as I used to." I show him the tiny scar on my knee.

Cristiano rotates his shoulder again as he tries to relieve the numbness in his hand. "I know you're right. I just have to figure it out. I can't continue to be in this much pain. It makes my daily life almost intolerable."

"For now, why don't you hand over Kennadie? I'll give her a bath and put her to bed."

"You know, when you told me you never wanted to be a mom, I assumed you were terrible with children — but you're not."

I try not to let my irritation show. "I like other people's children fine — I just don't feel it's the right move for me."

After I grab a bath towel and take my niece from Cristiano, he walks up behind me and starts to rub the tension out of my neck. "I'm sorry, I didn't mean to hurt your feelings. I'm just trying to understand. You seem like such a natural at this — it's odd to me. Most women I know who don't want to be mothers have a difficult time relating to children. That doesn't seem to be the case with you."

Kennadie sees Brando playing on the floor and tries to take a dive out of my arms. "I'm too busy to have this conversation right now — but, we can talk about it later," I say as I hold Kennadie a little tighter. "Let's go get you clean. Your mommy and daddy don't need to know Cristiano fed you cheese puffs. We need to get rid of the evidence."

Kennadie laughs and pats my face as we all walk toward the bathroom.

⎯⎯•⎯⎯

As I gently close Kennadie's door, I try not to make a sound, I steel myself against the conversation yet to come. I don't know how I'm going to breach this topic with Cristiano. What I have to say tonight might damage our relationship beyond repair. The thought of losing him makes me profoundly sad. Meeting Cristiano is the best thing which ever happened to me. Now, I'm afraid it'll all go up in smoke.

I swallow hard and enter my bedroom where Cristiano has his knee propped up on pillows. He's reading a magazine about racing.

"Did she finally give up the fight?" Cristiano asks with a smile. "That little girl played hard. She'll sleep well tonight."

I grin at him. "Well, you *are* her favorite play toy. She can use you as a jungle gym or a hobbyhorse, and you make all sorts of funny noises — what isn't there to love?"

Cristiano buffs his fingernails against his chest, "I always did have a knack for charming the ladies."

I nod as I say, "I can't really argue. You have been known to charm the socks and many other things off of me."

"If I'm so charming, why do you look like I'm about to bite your head off?" Cristiano asks as he pats the bed beside him.

This is bad. My stomach is churning like I've been on a roller coaster and we haven't even started our conversation yet. "I'm afraid," I admit as I remove my shoes and socks.

"Afraid of what? Me?" Cristiano asks with a confused expression on his face.

I climb into bed next to him. "You don't frighten me, but I am afraid of your reaction to what I'm going to say. I haven't had this conversation with a man in a while — because quite frankly I'm tired of men trying to decide what's best for me. Eventually, I started censoring myself, when I would go out on dates. I stopped bringing the topic up altogether. I'm just tired of the judgment."

Cristiano still looks anxious. "If this is about having kids, I wasn't trying to judge you, I just want to understand where you're coming from," he insists.

"I face so much criticism from everyone over my choice not to be a parent, that even things which are said to be nice start to feel like you're slapping me in the face. I know you probably don't agree with my choice, but I can't change the way I feel."

"If I knew why you made this decision, it might be easier for me to understand."

"I don't even know if I can explain it to you," I respond helplessly.

"Can you try? I like you a whole lot more than I ever thought I was capable of — especially since I have been burned. For the first time in my life, I feel like I'm truly part of a couple. You and I seem like two sides of the same coin. Our relationship feels different to me than any other I've been in. I want to figure out what makes you tick. It's such a big part of you, I want to understand."

"Bear with me, this is going to get a little long and convoluted. I've never told anyone the whole story before."

"Take your time," Cristiano coaxes.

I draw my knees up to my chest as I start to bare my soul. "I always enjoyed being around kids. I had fun being the one in charge and taking care of them. My mom and I would go to the homeless shelter and take little gift packages for the families there. That was my first rude awakening to the fact that kids don't always have two parents and a place to call home. It made me feel powerless. I wanted to be able to fix the world. I was angry when I couldn't."

"That seems natural."

"I was a teenager when my sister-in-law, Marquette, left Jasmine in a hot car trapped in her car seat. She killed my niece. It was such a waste."

Cristiano draws in a shaky breath as he absorbs my words.

I forge ahead with my story. "I had a special relationship with Jasmine. She was the coolest little girl ever. She was smart and wise beyond her years. It felt more like we were sisters than an aunt and a niece. She would call me up on the phone just to talk to me, and we would go get our nails and hair done. She was always ecstatic to see me. It made me feel about ten feet tall. In a blink, she was gone. I was devastated."

"Oh Jor," Cristiano murmurs under his breath, "I'm

so sorry."

"Everyone was concerned about Jaxson. They totally should have been — but no one realized how close I was to Jasmine. I fell into a deep depression. Everything started falling apart for me. I got into trouble at school and let my grades slip. I didn't care about anything anymore."

"I can't imagine — that must've been heartbreaking." He pulls me a little closer into his embrace.

I nod. "It was. I vowed never to get attached to another human being again in my life."

"I don't blame you" Cristiano says.

"Eventually, I went away to college, but I didn't have a way to support myself. My mom always worked hard at my grandfather's optical shop. Unfortunately, there was never a lot of money to go around. I had to find something I was good at. The only thing I had ever really done was babysit kids. So, I signed up for an *au pair* service, figuring I could find a job which would pay me some money and maybe provide a place to live."

"That sounds like a smart strategy. I've heard those jobs can sometimes pay pretty well."

"I'll admit, I wasn't hurting for money back then — most of the families treated me quite well. Even so, I was dismayed by what I found. I expected the families to be like mine — except with more money to throw around. A lot of the people I thought had the perfect life from the outside, had truly terrible lives once you scratched through the veneer of social standing and money. Some of the parents I worked for didn't care about their kids.

They treated them like they were chess pieces on a board they could pick up and move around at will. The parents were fine if they wanted to show their children off. Day-to-day parenting was left to me."

"That's awful."

Jordan glances out the window and shakes her head. "It was … but it was even more than that. A lot of these kids were afraid of their parents and would come to me instead. I was fired from a job once because the little three-year-old preferred me over her mother. But, the kid's choice made perfect sense because the mother was hardly ever around. The mother was virtually a stranger to this little girl, and the father worked all the time."

"That's so sad, my mom worked as a hairdresser and my dad as a city employee, but Ana Sofía and I never lacked for love."

"I felt the same way. I was shocked to find out that I was happier growing up than many of these rich kids I worked with. The first year I worked as a nanny, I was shuffled between families as I tried to build up my resume and get a more permanent position. I saw a lot of questionable behavior, but I wasn't allowed to say anything."

Cristiano kisses the top of my head but doesn't say anything. "Eventually, I got placed with these adorable twins. Even though I had sworn I would never love another child again, these kiddos managed to wiggle their way into my heart. They had a younger sibling, and without warning, he got an aggressive form of bone cancer and was dead within a month and a half. I had nursed him through the chickenpox and countless bouts of the flu. To lose another child I considered to be like my own was the final straw."

"Jordan, it wasn't your fault," Cristiano murmurs softly as he wipes a tear from my cheek.

"Sometimes that's difficult for me to remember." I lean into his hand. "I guess that's when I was reminded even though you may be a parent, nothing is permanent. You can't trust the love you have for your kids to save everything and make the world better. It doesn't work that way. Terrible things happen to children and grown-ups can't necessarily stop that. Love is not enough. If I took the losses so hard as an aunt and as a nanny, I can't imagine how devastating it would be to lose a child. I just can't take the risk."

"I can see why you would be reluctant to open your heart up again."

"I got tired of grieving for the children who I couldn't help or the ones who passed away. It was safer to choose a different lifestyle," I explain with a shrug.

"I'm sorry other people question your choices without knowing why you made them. Thank you for trusting me enough to share the whole story. It helps me understand more about what is happening."

"That's just it … I don't feel like sharing my story with just anyone. Yet, everyone feels the right to judge me for my decision. They have no idea why choosing not to be a parent is the right choice for me."

"The people who feel free to share their opinions with you should probably keep them to themselves. Being a parent should not be a competition sport. You should have kids because you love them — not because they are a possession to get or a win to put on a scoreboard."

"How do you feel about all this?" I ask with fear in my voice.

Cristiano shrugs with a pained expression. "I don't really know. I think it's going to take some time for me to process everything you said."

"Let me guess … you can't handle the idea of maybe never having kids with me. It'd be okay if we were just casually dating, but if things get serious, you're going to dump me like yesterday's old coffee, right?" I ask bitterly.

Cristiano holds up his hand. "Whoa! Don't put words in my mouth — I said, I need to think about it. You just dumped a whole load of stuff on me. I have to sort through it and figure out how it fits in my life. That doesn't mean I'm planning to ditch you."

"It doesn't necessarily mean you're not."

A huge tear escapes from the corner of my eye and rolls down my face. Cristiano wipes it away with his thumb. "We'll figure this out. I promise."

The sound of my phone scares us both. I dive for it because it is Jaxson's ringtone. "What took you so long to call? Is Donda okay?" I ask frantically.

I hear my brother's breath catch as he says, "No, she's not all right. She has endocarditis —"

"Indo what?" I ask.

"Endocarditis. Basically, she has an infection in a valve of her heart. At the moment, she is fighting for her life. She needs to have her valve repaired in her heart tonight. They're prepping her now. I need you to watch

Kennadie for a little while longer. Is that all right?"

"Of course — for as long as you need, Cristiano and I have it handled. Go be with Donda and let her know it'll be all right. I don't want her to be worried about anything other than getting better."

"Thank you, Sissy. I love you," my brother says, using our childhood nickname.

"I love you too," I whisper as he hangs up the phone.

Cristiano pulls me into his lap and nestles me against his chest. "It will be all right. Donda is strong. She is a fighter, and there is no way she'll give up on Kennadie and Gabriel."

I choke on a sob. "I can't lose anyone else. I know I didn't like Donda at first, but now I love her like a sister. I never wanted anything to happen to her. I can't imagine my life without her."

"No one is going anywhere, including me," Cristiano assures me as he brushes my hair out of my eyes and kisses my cheek.

Chapter Sixteen

Cristiano

"I WANT TO THANK you for being flexible," Jaxson says as he hands me a cup of coffee. "It means a lot to Donda and me that you were willing to adjust your schedule."

"Your sister is the best thing to ever happen to me. I consider you guys to be like family. I'm honored to help."

"How is your boss taking this?" Jaxson asks as he studies me.

"Well, it turns out my intern from the university is quite a talented broadcaster. Rowden doesn't even seem to notice I'm gone." I answer with a shrug. "I may or may not have a job to return to. At this point, I'm not really worried about it. Jordan needs me here, so here is where I am."

"Your dedication to my sister is impressive. It's been a long time since anyone's treated her with dignity and respect. I used to worry about her a lot, but I fret a lot less now that you're in her life."

I didn't realize how much Jaxson's approval means. He's important to Jordan, so it's great to have his blessing. The tips of my ears turn red. "Thanks, I appreciate it. Enough about me … how is Donda feeling?"

"She's already lobbying to get back to work. This reminds me of when we first met. Back then, I was trying to keep her off her bad leg. She wouldn't stay still to save her soul. Her rehab took far longer than it needed to. Hopefully, this time she's learned her lesson about following doctor's orders. This surgery was a lot more dangerous than a meniscus repair."

"Donda doesn't seem to be the type of person to lounge around on the couch willingly, so this must be incredibly frustrating for her."

"Not to mention that she absolutely hates to take any kind of medication because of her past drug use."

My eyes widen. "Are you telling me she had a valve replaced in her heart and she's not using pain medication? That's pure grit right there."

"Yeah, she didn't want to risk becoming addicted again, so she elected to handle all this with nothing stronger than ibuprofen."

"Wow!" I exclaim. "I always thought your wife was impressive, but this takes it to a whole new level."

Jaxson chuckles softly. "Welcome to my world."

While I'm drinking my coffee in a comfy beanbag chair beside the breakfast bar, Kennadie comes up and jumps on my arm as if it's a hobby horse. I feel a searing heat travel from my shoulder to my fingertips. It feels like someone set my nerves on fire.

Instinctively I reach out with my other arm to catch the baby before she falls, but Jaxson beats me to it. "Whoa, little cowgirl, you can't just ambush people, you'll hurt somebody," he warns his daughter as he redirects her to another toy.

I break out in a cold sweat as pain flies up and down my arm like an electrical charge. "Too late," I hiss as I gingerly set down my cup of coffee. "I think your cowgirl took me out."

Jaxson takes one look at my expression. "Oh crap! Let me get you some ice and I'll get Gabriel to watch Kennadie. I need to get you to my ortho guy. Are you up to staying around here for a while or should I try to get you home to Colorado?"

I glance over toward the wall where a stunning picture of Jordan is hanging. I raise my eyebrow in question as I ask, "What do you think?"

Jaxson shoots me a quick grin. "Oregon and my ortho it is."

"You have an ortho guy? But aren't you a doctor? Why would you have your own ortho guy when this is your specialty?"

"Because ethically, I'm not allowed to operate on my family members. It's not good practice. Don't you have an ortho you're currently seeing?"

"No, I lost my access to those doctors when I quit racing. I haven't gone to an orthopedic doctor since I've been in Aspen. Based on the way they messed my shoulder and knee up, I can't say I'm sad. Technically I'm not family, can't you just diagnose me?"

"You are so near to being family. It would be skating a line I'm not comfortable with. I would rather you be in the hands of Dr. Hopewell. Doug is very talented and probably better at doing arthroscopic procedures than I am. So, I've trusted Donda with him, and Gabriel too. If I trust my own family members to this doctor, I can count on him to do a good job on you too."

"Okay, I don't have the strength to figure this out anymore. I'll just take your recommendation. I feel like I'm about to throw up."

"You must be going into shock. Let me grab a basin for you." As we walk past the stairway, Jaxson yells out, "Gabriel! I need you on deck to watch Kennadie. She's supposed to be dropped off at daycare at noon. Can you handle that? I have to run Cristiano to the hospital, can you let your mom know what's going on?"

"Sure, Dad," Gabriel responds over the music playing in his room.

Jaxson grabs a coat from the coat tree and his keys off the rack. "Let's go. I want to see what we can do to reduce the swelling in your arm."

"Wait! I haven't even had a chance to tell Jordan."

"I'll send her a text from the hospital."

"Don't. Jordan will have a heart attack. Let's wait until we see what the doctor says."

"I can almost guarantee you they'll want to go in and repair your shoulder. It was dicey before you injured it today, and now it's probably far worse."

"Oh great! Not what I wanted to hear. I've got so many trips lined up I could fund a small country with what I spend on airfare."

"Well, you might have to postpone them. I think my daughter did a number on you."

"What does she weigh? All of thirty pounds, if that —"

"Thirty-two, actually. That goes to show you what a mess you were in to start with if my munchkin can completely shred your shoulder." Jaxson grins at me. "Hey, you might like Dr. Hopewell better than you like me. The nurses claim he's more handsome," he teases with a wink.

"Funny. I just wish I was in your hands and no one else's. It's difficult for me to trust doctors because of the surgeries that went wrong the first time I had them."

"Well, if it makes you feel any better, I can scrub in and observe."

I nod tightly. "Yeah, I think I'd like that."

⸺◦⸺

"You know, if you wanted to hang out with me longer, we could have come up with a less painful plan," Jordan jokes as she gets me some more ice chips.

"That's the thing — not much planning went into this, I promise. One minute I was having coffee with your brother, the next minute, they were putting me under for surgery."

"I told you to get it repaired earlier, but you wouldn't listen to me. You just wanted to be a tough guy," Jordan chastises.

"I already told your brother you'd diagnosed me.

You were pretty much spot on except for the ungodly amount of scar tissue I had in my shoulder. No wonder it felt like I was moving it through shards of glass. They showed me pictures they took while they were doing the operation, it looked like hamburger meat in there."

"I'm glad Jaxson could help you," Jordan dumps out my ice pack and puts new ice in it. She hands it back and says, "I guess sometimes it helps to have contacts at the hospital."

"I guess I got an assist from the weather. Some guy in Eastern Oregon, who couldn't catch a plane to get here to have his hip replacement surgery. I guess the storm was too severe. So, I guess Mother Nature and your brother conspired together to get me under the knife."

"I hate to ask you this, but have you even told your family what's going on?" Jordan asks with a raised eyebrow.

I shake my head and then regret the motion as I start to feel nauseous again. "No, I didn't have a chance. It was all over in the time it took me to blink."

"It only seems that way to you — for those of us waiting in the waiting room, it was three and a half hours. Every minute felt like an eternity. I've never prayed so hard in my life —well, not since Jasmine died I guess," Jordan says thoughtfully.

"While I was awake in the ER, I was doing my fair share too."

"So, are you planning to call your parents or do you want me to?"

"Well, considering they haven't met you yet, it might

be a good idea for me to make introductions first. After that, you and my mom can talk like old-school girls because that's what she always does with my friends."

"What about your sister?" Jordan asks, as she examines me carefully. "You look uncomfortable, are you taking your meds? Don't try to be a tough guy."

"Yes, I took my pain medication. This took more out of me than I expected."

"You're supposed to be resting, so I'll get you a new drink, and you can call your parents and let them know you had surgery and everything is okay. They'd probably appreciate it."

"Probably," I mumble as my eyes droop with fatigue.

"You look a little wiped out, do you want me to call your sister for you?" Jordan asks as she digs my phone out of my jacket pocket and hands it to me.

"That's probably not necessary, if it turns out to be something big, my parents will call her. I don't want to bother her at work. I'm not exactly sure what shift she's working this month, because they change from month to month."

"Okay, I'll give you some privacy so you can call your parents," Jordan offers as she grabs my empty glass and walks toward the kitchen.

"I appreciate the drink, but you don't need to stay away. My mom will want to see you anyway."

Jordan looks down at herself. "Why doesn't anyone want to see me when I'm dressed to the nines. Usually, when I have to meet someone new I look like some poster child for a discount store."

"My mom probably won't even notice the way you're dressed."

"Oh, you'd be surprised. Women notice these things, otherwise fashion designers like me wouldn't have a job," she adds with a grin.

Jordan tucks a blanket round me. "You should be sleeping."

"Let me call my parents first," I say as my phone falls to my chest.

"You know what? I'll take care of that for you. You seem a little too tired to deal with being social. No need to freak out everyone even more."

"Okay, thanks. I love you Jor —" I mumble.

* * *

Jordan carries a plate of quesadillas and salsa into the living room. She sets it down on the coffee table. "Hey, were you expecting company today?"

"No, I was planning to veg out in front of the television and watch some races I missed." I try to shift positions and reach the plate without jarring my shoulder. It seems simply breathing is enough to send a shock wave pain up my arm.

"Well ... I've only seen her pictures on Facebook, but I think your sister is sitting in my driveway."

"No way!"

"Way. I'm pretty sure it's her. Did you know she was coming?"

"No! I didn't. Ana Sofía and I haven't been on speaking terms for a while. I mean, we can manage to be civil to each other during family events, but we have history between us which won't quickly be forgotten."

"History?" Jordan asks.

"This isn't the right time to talk about it. Let's say, Ana Sofía has a different take on the world than I do. She felt inclined to believe the stranger over her own brother."

"I'm sorry. That must've hurt. Still, we all see the world through our own personal experiences made up of all our triumphs, tragedies, and fears. Maybe you just can't see what Ana Sofía does."

While I take a second to absorb Jordan's explanation, the doorbell rings. Jordan pauses at the door and looks over her shoulder. "Time for fence-mending?"

I grit my teeth as a wave of pain washes over me. Apparently, I haven't mastered the art of sitting up on my own without tweaking my shoulder. I glance over at Jordan. "I wasn't really planning to, but since when does my life go according to plan?"

"Welcome to the club," Jordan says as she picks Brando up and opens the door.

⬤●⬤

Ana Sofía is nervously flitting around the living room as she starts to pick up stray dishes and glasses from our impromptu pizza party. "I gotta hand it to you, little brother, you have a way with women. I can't believe Jordan is out getting you your favorite kind of ice cream after she already picked up pizza for you. You're all kinds of spoiled."

"I won't disagree. Jordan has been great for me."

"Really? I gotta be honest with you here — I think she's weird."

"Why do you say that?" I ask.

"Well, I guess I never thought I'd see you with someone who is so blindly ambitious."

"I don't see Jordan that way. She's not anything like she's being portrayed in the media."

"That's not what I mean. I don't even know what you're talking about. All I'm saying is — it's cool to have a career and all, but to put it ahead of having a family seems strange to me."

"Don't. You have no idea what you're talking about. You can't judge Jordan for her choices."

"I can and I will. I want you to end up with the right person. I'm just not sure Jordan is that woman."

"So, you just decided that without getting to know me first?" Jordan says from the doorway. She is carrying a cardboard drink caddy in one hand and a bag of groceries in the other. 'Hardly seems fair."

My sister blushes. "I'm sorry. I didn't mean for you to hear that."

"Believe me ... I totally understand. I have been in your shoes. I've made some unfair assumptions about my sister-in-law and I almost ruined my brother's life."

"That's what I'm trying to stop here," Ana Sofía says as she glares at me. She turns to Cristiano and says, "You know this will break Mom's heart. They are counting on grandchildren from you. You know I have fertility issues, and it's likely I'll never get pregnant. If you decide to not have children, our family line dies with you. Are you okay with that?"

"I didn't know you were having any issues. I haven't spoken to you other than to say Merry Christmas and Happy Thanksgiving in years. I hate that things are not working out the way you'd hoped. Still, it doesn't give you a right to judge Jordan for her choices."

"I think it does! I would give anything to be able to have children, and she is just throwing it all away. For what? So she can work harder at her job, travel, or have you all to herself? I don't know, but it seems a little selfish."

"Isn't it enough that your brother and I make each other happier than we've ever been in our whole lives? Why does the dream have to involve children? Maybe having kids is the right move for you, but why does everyone have to make the same choice?" Jordan asks.

"I can't believe you are so cavalier about this. What if someone ripped your dreams out from under you?" Ana Sofía snaps.

"There is nothing cavalier about my decision. I've thought through everything hundreds of times. I have my reasons." Jordan is on the verge of tears.

I adjust the pillow under my elbow as I look at my sister. "I know this is frustrating for you. I'm sorry for that, but I'm not sorry for my relationship with Jordan. Sure, I like kids. The simple truth is, I like Jordan more. I respect her right to make the decision she needs to be happy in life. That includes not having kids."

"Are you listening to yourself?" my sister challenges. "You always make rash decisions and then try to rationalize them later."

"Are we having a conversation about my decision-making now — or my decision-making back then?" I ask biting off each word as my anger rises.

"I guess a bit of both," Ana Sofía admits.

"Well, I was confident in my ability to make the right choice back then, and I still am today. I know you don't believe me but, I didn't do anything to that girl."

My sister puts down the stack of plates and silverware. She perches on the edge of the couch. "I'm sorry Cris, this apology should have come a long time ago. I'm sorry I didn't jump to your defense. It's just that the parasite's story was so similar to my roommate's experience in high school. I had a hard time separating the two. I know you wouldn't do anything like that."

"Thank you for saying so. I didn't know what to do when I lost the faith of my big sister. I don't always make perfect decisions, but there are lines I won't cross. If you ask me to choose between Jordan and having a relationship with my family, it is not likely to work out in your favor. I'm just letting you know."

"I hope you don't have a lifetime of regrets."

Jordan comes over and places her hand on my good shoulder in a show of support.

"I don't plan on it. I am looking forward to happily ever after. Jordan and I are just taking a different path to get there."

"I hope you find it, Cris. I want you to be happy. I

didn't come here to fight. I came here to try to make things better between us — not worse."

"Ana Sofía, please understand I'm not asking Cristiano to choose between his family and me. I just want people to understand that we have to lead our own lives," Jordan says gently.

"Am I so wrong to hope that you guys change your mind?" Ana Sofía asks Jordan.

The corners of Jordan's mouth lift up in a quirky smile. "I'll send you an invitation to the 'Jordan Needs a Baby' club. My mother and sister-in-law are founding members. The hope never dies —" Jordan teases.

"As long as you have an open mind …" Ana Sofía answers with a shrug.

Chapter Seventeen

Jordan

Shaking off my umbrella, I step through the doors of Gwen the Flower Petal'r. Even though Gwendolyn provided the flowers for my brother's wedding, this is the first time I've actually been in the shop. Donda told me her mom's shop was beautiful and quaint, but those words don't do it justice, I think as I look around. Gwendolyn comes out from a back room and greets "Jordan! What can I get you today? We have some new succulents … if you like those. They're fresh from the nursery. Or perhaps you would prefer orchids."

I blink at the barrage of questions. I pause for a moment as I sort through them. "I better hold off on the succulents until I have a place of my own. I don't want to overrun Donda with flowers. Besides, she has inquisitive children — both two legged and four — who get into everything."

"Good point. So, what can I help you with?" she inquires with a friendly smile.

"Your daughter thought you might have the answer

to my problem." I remove a piece of fabric from my purse and show it to her. "You wouldn't by any chance have any matching grosgrain ribbon, would you? I ran out of bias tape — but if you have ribbon, I have a bias tape maker."

"Knowing me, there is a reasonably good chance you'll find something here." She walks me over to a huge cabinet containing nothing but rows and rows of ribbon. Gwendolyn holds my fabric pieces up to the shelf. "I don't know about you, but I see a couple of matches here. It would be your personal preference. I think they both match well."

"The back of this piece is light, so I want the dark color, please. I want my quilt to have some contrast, if you know what I mean. I was afraid I wouldn't find anything, but this is perfect."

Gwendolyn smiles gently at me. "I like perfect. I'm so glad I could help you. How many yards do you need?"

"That's such a pretty color — can I just have the whole roll?"

"You sure can. How is your young man? Did Jaxson fix him right up? Your brother is such a talented doctor. You should be so proud."

"I am very proud of Jax. He wasn't able to do surgery on Cristiano because of our relationship, but he had one of his partners do it. Cristiano is feeling much better."

Gwendolyn studies me for a moment before she says, "You seem a little sad. I would think Cristiano's recovery would be good news. What's going on?"

I smile, but I have tears in my eyes. "You would think so, wouldn't you? But I'm so confused about our relationship. I don't know what to do."

Gwendolyn looks up at the clock. "It's time for me to close. Let me put the sign on the door, and then we'll talk."

"I'll grab your sandwich board from the sidewalk by the street," I offer as I set my purse down on her counter.

"Thank you, dear."

"It's no problem at all." I go to retrieve the sign.

By the time I come back, Gwendolyn has all the signs in the window turned off and has a box of Kleenex and a couple bottles of water on a decorative tray. At my questioning look, she answers, "Just a precaution. We have lots of Girlfriend Posse meetings in here, and things can get a little emotional. So, I've learned to be prepared."

Gwendolyn gathers up the items and motions for me toward her. "Follow me. We'll get everything sorted out."

She takes me to an out-of-the-way corner of her store which has a park bench and luscious tropical plants around it. I hear a fountain in the background.

"Oh wow!" I gasp when I see it. "How do you get any work done knowing you have this little oasis? I would be tempted to camp out and read books all day."

Gwendolyn sets the tray down on a side table as she says in a stage whisper, "I'll tell you a secret — some days when it's slow in here, I do just that."

"How could you not? The pull would be irresistible. If you don't mind, if I ever get my own home again, I'm going to replicate this little area. It is so peaceful."

"I know you will have that chance someday soon. My daughter was so happy with the clothing you made for her."

"I'm so touched."

"Have you ever considered opening your own boutique? There are lots of people in the world like Donda and Cristiano. I think your business would do really well."

"I'm thinking about it. But I'm not sure it's the right move. There are so many things to consider."

"From the look on your face, it seems perhaps the future of your career is not the only thing on your mind."

"That's because it's not — not by a long shot. I have so many things to figure out, I don't even know where to start."

"I have nowhere to be," Gwendolyn pats my knee sympathetically.

Touched by her kindness, I forge ahead. "Everything between us has been complicated by problems at work."

"Honey, it's not a relationship unless it's complicated. If everything was easy, you wouldn't value each other. If you'll remember, Denny met me right before I started my fight with cancer — talk about your less than perfect time to fall in love. I felt so guilty that I fell in love with him because I wasn't sure if I would survive my bout with lung cancer."

I wipe away a tear. "This isn't quite as serious as what you went through, but I feel guilty too. I decided a long time ago having children is not a path I want to pursue. When I made my decision, I didn't realize the impact it would have on my partner. I guess I should have, but I was so busy fighting with the people who disagree with me that it never occurred to me how much strain my decision puts on our relationship."

"That must be difficult," Gwendolyn murmurs.

"What if his sister is right? I don't want Cristiano to settle for a life with me if he wants to have kids — especially if it ruins his relationship with his family." I grab a tissue from the box and dab my eyes. "These are the kind of questions which keep me up at night."

Gwendolyn looks thoughtful as she asks. "What does Cristiano say about all of this?"

I shrug. "Real life has managed to get in the way. We haven't discussed it much. First Donda had her crisis with endocarditis, and then Cristiano got hurt. Not to mention the whole legal fight with my former boss. Cristiano has some issues going on at work too. We haven't even had a chance to sort it all out."

Gwendolyn nods. "I know how that works. It's easy to let life's challenges get in the way of what's important."

"Now, on top of everything else, there is this thing with Ana Sofía. She thinks I'm bad for her brother. Talk about karma … after the way I treated your daughter, I can't say I deserve better."

"That's all ancient history. Donda has let it go, I bet you could do the same. I don't know about you, but I don't cope well if I have things topsy-turvy in my life. With all the things you have up in the air, it must be hard to juggle it all. I don't envy you. Has Cristiano given you any indication about how he feels?"

"Yes! That's the most confusing part. He has been completely supportive of all of my decisions even under pressure from his family."

"I can tell you from personal experience, having your partner stand up for you is one of the most valuable things in a relationship."

"It is pretty amazing," I concede. "There's more... After his surgery, he told me he loved me. I don't know if it was a side effect of his medication, if he was just overtired, or if he really meant to say it. I'm too embarrassed to ask because how do you even bring that kind of thing up in casual conversation?" I let out a whoosh of air before I whisper, "What if he didn't mean what he said? I'd be crushed."

"It sounds as if you're falling in love too."

"Despite all the chaos, I think I am." It's been a long time since I've been brave enough to love someone. I take a long drink of water. "I don't know how this happened. Usually, I have my guard up."

Gwendolyn giggles as she replies, "Honey, after three husbands, the thing I have learned about love is we're not in control of when it strikes. Do you think that logically, I would go after my daughter-in-law's father? It was the furthermost thing from my mind. Still, every time I needed a friend, I found myself turning to Denny. He was a solid, loving presence in my life when I had gone years without. It seemed like one day, we were chummy friends and the next day I had fallen in love. To this day, I'm not exactly sure when it happened. But, it doesn't make our love any less real; everybody's love story is different."

"I suppose you're right, I can't plan this out like it's some pattern for an outfit. Life is too unpredictable for that."

"Have you told Cristiano how you feel?" Gwendolyn questions gently.

"No, I haven't really. I've definitely hinted though. Things have been so topsy-turvy in our lives that I haven't found a good time to lay it all out in black and white."

"I don't know what to tell you exactly, but I know there is never a truly bad time to tell someone you love them."

"Thanks for the talk," I reply as I embrace Gwendolyn. "I guess I have some serious decisions to make."

"Good luck."

"Thanks, I'll let you know what happens."

"I look forward to the update," Gwendolyn replies as she escorts me to the door and gives me a brief hug.

———◆———

All the way home, I turn over ideas in my head about the best way to tell Cristiano how I feel. I don't know if I should go for a casual-slip-of-the-tongue or if I should go for a more formal, romantic declaration with all the bells and whistles. To be honest, I haven't gotten to this point in my relationships before. I mean, I have dated and once I even moved in with a guy, but it didn't turn out the way I expected. I am more nervous than anything else. What if Cristiano thought about his choices and decided

I'm not worth it?

I take a deep breath and let it out as I pull my car into the driveway. I guess I'll play it by ear, because I don't know the best way to tell him how I feel.

As soon as I open the front door, I can tell something is wrong. Cristiano is laying on the couch with the laptop balanced on his lap, trying to operate it with one hand while he screams obscenities at the screen.

I rush over to him and prop a pillow under the laptop before it falls on the floor. "Does that help?"

"You'll probably save the computer, but that's not what the issue is here. Your former boss is a freakin' witch. She doesn't know who she's messing with. I'm sorry, you need to call your attorney and shut this crap down. She shouldn't be allowed to do this. You didn't destroy her fashion line, you left your job. I don't know why she feels like she has the right to decimate everyone's life around her. I don't understand why she thinks she has a legal leg to stand on. This is crazy — like all the way to *loco* town —"

Cristiano is so agitated I am afraid he'll hurt his shoulder if he doesn't calm down. I take the computer off his lap and sit down on the couch beside him.

"What is going on?" I ask again trying to cut through his tirade.

"Oh, my Gosh! How can you not know?" he exclaims incredulously. "Crap, I have to be the one to tell you."

"Tell me what?" I ask insistently

"It's ugly."

Seeing the rage on his face makes my heart sink. This was everything I feared when it became apparent Mishka put a bull's-eye on my back. I tried to warn Cristiano before we ever got together it might be dangerous for his career to hang around me. I sigh as I stand up and grab the laptop computer and sit back down beside him. "Where are your headphones?"

"Brando got a hold of them and used them as a chew toy, so we'll all have to listen to her garbage at least one more time. I'm telling you … that woman is not right in the head."

"I've known that for a while. I've been covering for her and trying to hold the business together. Mishka's mental instability is not news to me. For some reason, she has become a caricature of herself."

"Do you suppose she's on something?" Cristiano asks. "That would be about the only explanation that would account for what you're about to see."

"Please stop," I plead. "You're scaring me. I don't know if I even want to see it."

I watch with apprehension as the video restarts. To my horror, Mishka has somehow discovered Cristiano and I are dating. She again accuses me of stealing all of her designs and many of her clients. She cites Cristiano as an example. She claims I poached him right under her nose.

By the time the video finishes running, my hands are shaking so much the screen on the laptop is trembling. Rage courses through my body like an energy drink.

I look up at Cristiano. "How in the world can she do this? Isn't it illegal to smear someone's reputation with facts you haven't verified as true? She can be mad at me all she wants to, but she needs to leave you out of this." My face grows hot with anger.

"Now you know how I feel when she goes after you. She has no reason to destroy you. You guys aren't even competing for the same market — as far as I know, you're not planning to go after any big stars in Hollywood, correct?"

I blow out a breath. "I haven't even decided if I'll stay in the fashion business. Madison has given me some options to use my journalism degree. As much as I love designing clothes, there's something to be said for completely avoiding anything to do with the fashion industry."

"Don't get me wrong, I think what you do is incredibly important. Even so, part of me wonders if you wouldn't be better off in an entirely different field," Cristiano punches the couch pillow with his good arm. "This pisses me off like you wouldn't believe. Why can't people mind their own business?"

I study the computer screen for a few more moments before I say, "Do you ever wonder who posts this garbage for her? Let me tell you, Mishka might be brilliant with textiles and design, but she doesn't really have any computer skills to speak of. She can barely send me a text message. Someone has to be posting all this crap for her."

Cristiano shudders. "That makes it even worse. Not only is she making garbage up, but she's also spending money to spread it. It's just wrong."

I close the computer and lay it on the coffee table

in front of Cristiano. I stand up and walk around the room as I try to process what's happened. I bury my head in my hands for a moment before I say, "I guess I'll give CJ a call. She'll know how to handle all this — or at least I hope she does."

CHAPTER EIGHTEEN

CRISTIANO

"IF YOU DON'T KNOW something, don't guess. Just say you don't know or you can't remember. Stick to the facts — but let people know how you felt," CJ Wells, Jordan's attorney, instructs me as a crew member clips on a mic pack. "Don't let the microphone make you nervous. It will pick up your voice fine. You won't need to yell."

I raise an eyebrow and smile at her. "I have done a little TV in my life. Though this studio is a bit of an upgrade compared to my usual stomping grounds."

My slightly snarky statement seems to bring CJ up short. "Oh, right. I knew that. I'm just focusing on other stuff right now."

The attorney turns to Jordan. She seems a bit frazzled. "Are you comfortable with your decision not to wear body makeup?"

Jordan nods. "The whole point of this session is for Cristiano and me to show the audience our true selves. If I'm going to stop wearing body make-up, this is as good a time as any to do 'a big reveal' as they say."

Madison steps forward and shakes my hand. "Thanks for agreeing to do this today. I'll ask you some softball questions to get you used to the format and then we'll talk about more complicated things."

"Complicated how?" I press.

"Obviously, you know I'm a big fan of your girlfriend. She has made my husband's life much more comfortable. He can work out in the barn now without his clothing irritating his stump. I won't do anything to destroy Jordan's career. I'll try to highlight the differences between Jordan and Mishka. My audience can draw its own conclusions. I won't ask questions which invite you to run Mishka down into the ground. I merely want to help get your story out and highlight Jordan's skills."

"So, no gotcha questions?" I ask. "I used to get those all the time when I was on the racing circuit."

Madison chuckles softly. "At this point, I don't anticipate that they will be gotcha questions. Feel free to jump in if you feel like Jordan is struggling with a question."

Something on set beeps and Madison checks her mic pack. "I need to go check this with production. I'll be right back."

Suddenly, everyone has left the room except Jordan and me. I reach out and squeeze her hand. "Are you doing okay?"

Jordan shoots me a timid grin. "I've been better, but I'll be happy when all this is behind us. I don't like feeding the media engine."

I reach up and brush her hair out of her eyes. I wish

I could kiss her, but I don't want to mess up her makeup. "This is more than just feeding the media machine. You are trying to get your side of the story out. It's been completely ignored for months. So, if Mishka's voice is the only one speaking, hers is the story the public is going to believe. We have to put our own spin on things or the public will decide you don't care."

"Oh … I care more than you can possibly imagine. It infuriates me that she feels like she has the right to destroy me. I helped to build her into what she is, so she should know I wouldn't roll over and take this."

CJ steps back on stage. "Jordan, I understand this is frustrating, but you need to try to play it a little closer to the vest. You don't want to come across to your potential fans or potential jurors as being petty, spiteful and narcissistic."

A horrified expression crosses Jordan's face as she asks, "Do I sound like that? I just want to tell my side of the story-without weird PR spin. I think I'm standing on pretty solid facts."

CJ nods. "If the facts weren't on your side, you and I would not be having this conversation. Defamation cases are notoriously hard to pursue. I don't take them lightly. Now, it's our turn to put your side of the story out to the public. So far, they haven't heard anything about it. Therefore, they assume Mishka's story is true."

CJ pauses for a moment before she says with deliberate emphasis, "*However*, just because you're telling your side of the story, you do not have the right to go after Mishka for what she has done to you. If you do that, it weakens our defamation case. Please, both of you, stick to the facts and the questions Madison asks. I'm hoping there's nothing she'll ask which would get us in trouble during litigation later — but, you need to be careful not to go off script and come unglued," she says looking directly at me.

"I understand. Just for the record — this crap makes my blood boil." I fidget with my tie.

Madison cringes when she walks in and sees my expression. She reaches out to straighten my offending neckwear. "Don't worry, all of us feel the same way. If you need to go to the gym with Trevor or one of the other guys when you're done to hit some heavy bags, be my guest. But here, we'll stay on the straight-and-narrow. I am not running one of those sleazy tabloid shows here."

I take a deep breath and then twist my torso to stretch out my body. "I swear, I'll be on my best behavior."

This time Madison laughs out loud. "I have a friend who used to cover the unusual sports circuit. He was well aware of your outside-of-the-competition ring antics. So, I'd advise you to shoot for your better-than-best behavior. I've heard what your usual best behavior covers."

"Point taken," I answer with an embarrassed grin. "I wonder if my past will ever stop biting me in the butt."

Madison looks up at a gentleman wearing a jean jacket. "It looks like Lee is ready for us. It's showtime!"

Jordan clutches her chest briefly. "I'm sorry, I didn't expect this to be so terrifying. I hope it's worth it!"

"It'll be fine, Jordan. I am about as friendly a journalist as you could run across. I'll be gentle, I promise."

Jordan blushes. "I know, Madison. I guess I'm more than a little peeved that I even have to go on television to defend myself. This is all crazy."

"I know better than most that the world is full of crazy. The goal is to navigate through it as best you can."

The stage manager, Lee, adjusts Jordan's mic clip. He turns to Madison. "Good to go, Mrs. Black."

Madison nods slightly as she watches the stage manager.

"Good afternoon. I don't know what the weather is like where you live, but here in the Pacific Northwest, it's a glorious fall day. Days like today always make me itch for a new wardrobe. That's why I am so happy to have fashion designer Jordan Shepherd with me. She brought one of her favorite clients, Cristiano Romero, with her today. Welcome to the two of you," Madison gestures toward us.

It is quite strange to see Madison functioning in a professional capacity. The last time I saw her, she was trying to get gum out of her daughter's hair. We've even mucked out her barn together.

"Cristiano, not to belabor the obvious, but you are a tall guy with shoulders made for playing football — as my grandma was fond of saying," Madison remarks as she lets her eyes roam over me.

"Yeah, I've been big like this since about my freshman year of high school."

Madison murmurs her sympathy as she remarks, "That must make it difficult to buy clothes."

"You have no idea. If I buy clothes to fit my broad shoulders, they are much too large everywhere else. If I fit them around my waist, things are far too tight across my shoulders."

"It must be incredibly difficult for you when you try to go shopping. Is that how you met Jordan?"

"It is. I wasn't thrilled when I was told to go visit a fashion designer. Wearing jackets of any kind can be a challenge for me, but it seems the fancier the clothes, the more uncomfortable they are for me."

Madison looks me over from head to toe. "Well … you look great today —"

"Before I met Jordan, I didn't look half as good. She has done the impossible. She designs clothing which actually fits. Between my time in front of the camera as a reporter covering the X-Games and the amount of time I spend attending charity events, I spend an ungodly amount of time in a suit. It's nice to be able to move freely."

"That's great! How did you find Jordan?"

I catch Jordan's eye and smile. "That part happened quite by accident. Jordan was working for another designer. She was having an exceptionally rotten day, and she ended up resigning from her job right in front of me."

"I bet that was awkward," Madison comments.

"It was a little strange, I'll give you that. I can't say I would've done anything differently. After listening to a few snippets of conversation, it was clear Jordan's supervisor didn't respect her talent."

"Well, did you step in and stand up for her?"

"Not right away," I confess. "After Jordan left, I met with her supervisor. Mishka Silk was the person my company recommended I see about formal wear. After trying to deal with Mishka for a few minutes, I could empathize with Jordan. Ms. Silk simply wasn't listening to me. She was trying to make me feel inferior because fashion is not my thing. It didn't take me long to conclude Mishka was not the designer for me."

"That must have caused quite a scene," Madison remarks. "Word on the street is Mishka does not like to be crossed."

"I suppose that's true enough. She threatened to destroy the careers of both Jordan and me. Based on what I've seen on television recently, it seems she's sticking to her word."

"So, you're saying all of the interviews casting you and Jordan in a very bad light are just retaliation because Jordan left her job?" Madison asks intently.

I shrug. "I don't know for certain because I can't see what's going on in Ms. Silk's brain. However, I do know she threatened both of us. Mishka promised to destroy us. It appears she is well on her way."

"That must be incredibly frustrating. You haven't spoken out in the media before, but I'd like to give you a chance to speak today. If there's anything you need to let the audience know, this is the time to share."

Running my hand down my face in complete

frustration, I say, "Anybody who knows me knows that this is not my style. I'm much better as part of a team or behind-the-scenes. This public persona outside of racing is new to me. I was nervous to go into a design shop. I didn't know what to anticipate, but I didn't expect to see one professional dressing down another as abruptly as Mishka was doing to Jordan. I have been part of several cycling teams, and even our most stringent coaches never talked to us the way this designer was talking to her protégé."

"As you know, there have been some pretty wild accusations flying around in the media. Did you see Jordan take anything with her when she left?"

"Only some photo frames of her family. She left everything else behind."

"Since it was clear to you that working with Mishka Silk was untenable, what was your next move?" Madison prompts.

"After the showdown in the middle of Mishka's shop, I still needed something to wear to the Sports Heroes with Heart's benefit. I looked Jordan up on social media and found a way to reach her."

Madison turns to Jordan, "What happened when Cristiano contacted you?"

Jordan smiles as she recalls the encounter at her brownstone. "I was surprised, certainly. Shocked was more like it — but then Cristiano issued a challenge I couldn't refuse. He told me he didn't believe it was possible to design something which was both formal and comfortable. Even though I was in the middle of moving to Oregon when all of this happened, I just couldn't turn down his dare."

"I know this whole matter is ugly, but I have to address the controversy that's out there. I hope you understand," Madison says with a gentle smile.

"I'd rather not be dealing with it at all," Jordan admits. "I haven't done anything wrong —"

Madison gives Jordan a sympathetic look "I know this is frustrating, but I have to ask, were any of the designs you are using in your new business Mishka's?"

"Absolutely not! I don't work that way. I worked in the industry for a long time. I know it takes incredibly hard work to be a designer. I would never steal another designer's designs. It goes against everything I am."

"I understand. But, Ms. Silk has made some serious allegations against you. Do you want to respond?"

"I really have nothing to say about Mishka's comments about my personal life. At one point, we were friends. I helped her build her business from the ground up. I want to see her succeed — I want both of us to do well."

"You know Mishka is publicly stating quite the opposite. She says without her help and designs, you would be nothing," Madison states.

"She can claim that all she wants to, but it doesn't mean it's true," Jordan responds with an exasperated sigh.

Even though I know Madison is trying to be helpful, it's incredibly difficult for me to leave the accusations unanswered. I lean forward and add, "If you don't mind, I would like to tell you about what Jordan has done for me. Your viewers can make up their own minds.

Jordan didn't come with any predetermined plans. She did a thorough job of sizing me up and asking what would work. I gave her a list of things that I liked and didn't like. From that, she created some of the most comfortable clothes I've ever worn. I was involved every step of the way and saw her progress. She can tell you a funny story about the time I mistook her muslin pattern for the real suit. Jordan had quite a laugh at my expense."

Madison laughs softly. "I would imagine so."

Looking directly at the camera, I continue, "I don't know about all of you, but before I met Jordan, I had no idea what was involved in designing custom clothes. It's actually a very intricate process. I've also discovered Jordan is conscientious, careful, and exacting. She's also wildly creative and helpful."

"Helpful? You mean because she finished your suit for your event?" Madison asks.

"It's true. Jordan pretty much saved me from embarrassing myself at the Sports Heroes with Heart Gala, but that's not what I'm talking about. She uses her skills to help people much needier than me, find clothes which fit and make them feel special. She's helping people with disabilities or those impacted by the march of time do things like participate in a wedding or work without the discomfort caused by their ill-fitting clothing. To me, that's much more important than making the cover of some fashion magazine. For those of you who have formed a poor impression of Jordan Shepherd because of the way she's been portrayed in the media, I can tell you that you don't know the real person."

Madison leans forward in her chair. "It sounds like

you've gotten close to Jordan Shepherd."

I shrug. "I don't deny that, but it's not the way it started out. I was looking for help to look decent on what was an important day in my career. Even though I have fallen in love with Jordan Shepherd, it doesn't mean what I say isn't true."

"That's sweet of you to say, what does Jordan say about the accusations against you?"

"Like anyone, she found them concerning until I explained the circumstances and the fact that I was completely exonerated. If Mishka was going to use my past against me, she needed to do her homework. Now, I haven't been an angel. I was on the racing circuit when I was a teenager. I did lots of stupid things. Although, under no circumstances did I ever sexually assault anyone. If I had done that, my mother and sister would've come after me with pitchforks. That's not who I am — then or now."

"It sounds like you've been through the wringer with the media," Madison remarks. "I'm surprised you agreed to talk to any of us today."

"Sometimes, you have to do the things which make you feel uncomfortable to stand up for yourself. That's exactly what Jordan did with Ms. Silk. It seemed like a no-brainer for me to share my side of the story. In case anybody has any doubts, I would've done this even if Jordan and I were not together. Right is right. I believe in taking a stand when you need to."

I notice Jordan wiping away a tear. Madison hands her Kleenex. "Wow! That's a good man you've got there, Jordan. Speaking of good things, can you give us a sneak peek at what you are working on next?"

"Well, you're looking at one of them. The suit I made Cristiano has some adaptations. He just had shoulder surgery, and his range of motion is somewhat limited. So, I changed the location of some of the pockets and used magnetic closures so he wouldn't have to struggle with the buttons."

Madison studies my suit a little more closely. "I would've never guessed that there were any adaptations to this garment. It looks like a regular sports jacket." She turns to Jordan. "I want to thank you for all the talent you have thrown in the direction of adaptive clothing. I hope you continue along this vein. I want to thank you and Cristiano for being my guest today. I learned a lot about you I did not know before. Hopefully, our viewers did too. Feel free to come back any time."

I lean forward and shake her hand. "Thank you so much for the opportunity."

The stage manager counts Madison down to commercial, and I let out a huge sigh of relief.

As the stage manager comes to take off our microphones, Madison leans forward and says, "Seriously guys, you killed it. My viewers will be inspired by how you turned a bad situation into a good one. They'll be fascinated by your love story too. It's like a modern day romantic novel."

"I definitely got lucky on the unluckiest day of my life. Thank you for giving us the opportunity to share our story," Jordan says as she stands up and stretches her legs.

The stage manager approaches and addresses Jordan, "I heard what you said. I think what you're doing is great. Do you ever work with kids?"

"I haven't had the opportunity to do that yet, but it doesn't mean I couldn't," Jordan answers.

"Well, my grandson has autism, and he is having a hard time with the buttons. I wondered if maybe you could use the same kind of magnet things to make it a little easier for him. He'll be hard to work with because he has his favorite kind of clothing and won't wear much else. I don't know if it will work for what you need. But I thought I would ask —"

Jordan smiles. "One of the things I've learned in this business is to be flexible. Why don't you give me your contact information and I'll get a hold of you and see what we can do?"

Lee shakes Jordan's hand vigorously. "Thank you so much. My daughter will be so excited to hear there might be something we can do to help little Dougie."

Jordan laughs a little at his enthusiasm. "Really, it's no problem at all. It's why I'm working hard to build JS Couture."

Lee flushes a shade of dark red. "It might be wrong of me to say this, but ma'am, I for one am very happy you walked away from your other job. I think you found your true calling in the world. I'm glad you stood up for yourself. I wish more people would do that. Everybody is just trying to do the same thing as everyone else. I wish things could go back to the way they were before."

"What do you mean, Lee?" Madison asks with open curiosity.

"Back in my day, if you were good at something,

you stuck to that thing and shared your gifts with other people. It's the way we were. If someone was mechanical, everyone took the car to them. If another person did a great job at house painting, they were the person we hired. These days, everyone is trying to be everything to everybody. I don't think it works so well. So, I'm glad to see you followed your passion, Ms. Shepherd."

"Please, call me Jordan. Thank you for telling me about your grandson, I'll try to do my best to come up with something to meet his needs."

I put my arm around Jordan's waist. "If Jordan says she'll solve a problem, she will. Don't worry about it. Your grandson will be the most decked-out kid in his school. She's just that good."

Jordan tears up. "Thank you for the vote of confidence. These days, my self-esteem has been a little shaky."

"I'm sorry Mishka has turned your life into this, but I was proud of you on the first day of this ordeal, and I'm a bigger fan now," I comment, as I brush a kiss against her temple.

CHAPTER NINETEEN

JORDAN

"You're quiet today, did you get blowback from our interview?" I ask as I try to decipher Cristiano's body language. Pensive is not usually a word I would associate with him, but today it seems to fit. He has his gaze pinned on the road ahead. Traffic is pretty heavy for the weekend as we head up 1-5 toward my mom's house.

"No, not really … at least I don't think so. Jubilee and Rowden are out of town this week, so we haven't had a chance to talk. The guy directing the show while they are gone is great. We are communicating well, and the conflict which often goes with working with Rowden isn't there. This guy is a true fan of sports and has been completely supportive of my decisions about what to cover. It's a nice change."

"Why do you look like somebody kicked your puppy?" I ask as I reach out to grab his free hand when he changes his grip on the steering wheel.

Cristiano heaves a heavy sigh. "I don't know. As great as it's been to work with Scott, it underscores the disagreements I have with my current directing team. I guess I didn't fully realize how difficult things had become between Rowden and I until I worked with someone else. It's the kind of partnership Rowden and I had in the beginning. I'll have to make some hard decisions soon. It won't be pretty."

"I know a little something about giving up everything you're comfortable with and launching a new life."

"I know. That weighs heavily on me too. I wish I was as brave as you and could throw away what I've built and stand on principle. Though, I don't know if it's a good idea for both of us to have our careers up in the air."

I frown at Cristiano and my spine stiffens. "I'll handle it regardless of what you do with your job. If nothing else, I'll go sell earrings at the mall if I need to. I'll do what I have to do to survive. Whatever you do, don't hold yourself back on my account."

"I know. I'm just not sure where to go from here. Some days, I wish I was still a naïve teenage BMX rider. Life seemed so much easier then. I just did my tricks or rode as fast as I could. There was only one goal — to beat everyone behind you. I miss the simplicity of it all."

"I know what you mean," I respond with a wistful sigh. "When I played basketball, it was just me and the basketball hoop. I could let my mind go blank. These days, my mind is rarely still. I'm always thinking and strategizing."

"To be young and clueless again," Cristiano says nostalgically.

"If you keep seeing my brother and the doctors in his practice, they'll turn you into a whole new human, and you will feel like a teenager again."

Cristiano rotates his shoulder around and then turns his hand palm side up. "You're not kidding! Look what I can do. The physical therapist was totally impressed by my range of motion. I don't think I've been this flexible since I broke my wrist during my second season."

"Yeah, that's one thing about hanging around my brother, he'll make sure you do your physical therapy. He's like a drill sergeant. When I hurt my knee, he was on me every day to do my strengthening exercises. In the end, he was right. My knee doesn't bother me much anymore."

"Your brother would kick my butt if I did anything to undo their handiwork. I'm tempted to take my bike out for a spin, but I'm afraid of Jaxson's wrath if I tweak something while I'm out there."

"You'll have a chance to ask him about it today. He's coming to lunch with my mom."

"How do you think it'll go today? I can't remember the last time I did the 'meet the parents' routine." He is trying to sound casual, but I can tell he is nervous. "I hope it goes better than your encounter with my family."

I roll my shoulder. "I don't know. Your sister was nice enough about it, I suppose. I don't know how I would react to someone like me if I was in her shoes."

"Jor, I was there, remember? Ana Sofía was downright rude to you. You're cutting her way more slack than I would."

"I feel sorry for your sister. She probably gets as much flack about her biological clock as I do. The only difference is she didn't get to make choices about whether her body works."

"I never thought about it that way. No wonder the whole topic pushes her buttons. Let's hope today has fewer fireworks."

"Take a deep breath, or you'll pass out. My mother will be thrilled you are there. I think she thought I was destined to stay single my whole life," I answer with a grin as I see him drumming his thumb on the steering wheel. "Besides, it's not a huge deal; you already know Jaxson, Donda, Gabriel, and Kennadie. It's just my mom. My mom is one of the greatest people I know. She beat cancer and never looked back."

"That's great. Tough for you though, I bet. When my grandma had cancer, my mom was beside herself."

"It was. It was scary there for a while, but I guess it was positive in one sense —"

"Really?" Cristiano asks skeptically.

I nod as I confirm, "Before Mom got sick, Jaxson and I fought like cats and dogs. Now look at us, I'm living in his house. A few years ago, I would've never thought it would be possible. But Mom's fight for her life put everything into perspective."

"I can imagine. I probably should work a little harder to patch things up with Rowden and Jubilee."

"Hopefully, you and Rowden will be able to sort things out. From what I've gathered, he's like family to you."

"He is. He took me under his wing when I was still a racer. He helped me cope with the loss of my racing career and gave me a reason to get up every morning. I owe him a lot. That's why this tiff over the future of our show is so disturbing. We used to be able to work everything out. For some reason, it doesn't seem possible now."

"Have you asked him what's changed?" I ask.

"No, I guess I should probably do that," Cristiano concedes as he pulls his car into my mom's driveway. "That's an issue for another day — I need to survive this family dinner first."

"Really, it'll be fine, and you're going to be spoiled by my mom's cooking, I promise." However, even as I say the words, I can't help but feel a little anxious myself. This is the first time I've ever brought anyone home that I'm serious about. I hope it goes well. I don't want to have to choose between my family and Cristiano.

— • —

There isn't much conversation as everyone is busy eating. Being back around my mom's old-fashioned kitchen table makes me feel nostalgic and a little guilty. Even though she doesn't live far away from Jaxson, I don't get up here to see mom nearly enough.

Cristiano leans back in his chair and sighs. "Mrs. Shepherd, I don't believe I've ever eaten homemade fried chicken before," Cristiano says as he rubs his stomach. "It's one of the best things I've ever eaten."

"Why thank you, young man. Please call me Yvette. If you call me Mrs. Shepherd, I look around for my mother-in-law."

I wink at my mom. "Wait until you try my mom's chess pie. You might have to rethink your ranking."

"Yvette, I can see where Jordan gets her skills from. Thank you so much for dinner. Do you need some help with the dishes?" Cristiano offers.

"Oh, Jordan, you found yourself a keeper here. He'll be such a help when you two have children."

"Mom! Did you *really* have to bring that up? We were having such a great time."

"I thought maybe since you left the rat race in New York, you might've changed your mind. After all, Donda and Jaxson told me what a great job you did babysitting Kennadie. That girl is downright irresistible. If she can't get your biological clock ticking, you're hopeless."

"Mom, that's not the way all of this works. Wanting a baby isn't something you catch like a disease. I have always enjoyed children, but I don't feel the need to have any of my own. My life is full right now."

"What about what Cristiano needs?" my mom persists. "You guys would make beautiful babies. Did you ever think of that? What if he wants to be a father?"

Cristiano's spine stiffens, and I hear his breathing change. Tears gather in the corner of my eyes as I take a deep breath. "All of this has occurred to me. I worry about it all the time. I understand what I want isn't in line with most people's expectations, but it doesn't make me a bad person."

"I don't understand. Was I such a terrible mother that you don't want to be like me?" my mom asks with pleading eyes.

"Mom, don't be ridiculous. You were amazing. You brought Jaxson and me up under almost impossible circumstances. Look at Jaxson, he's a doctor, for Pete's sake. Obviously, you didn't do a bad job."

"Then why?" my mom asks with a complete look of befuddlement.

It seems like my mom and I have a variation of this argument every time I see her. I don't know what else I can do to explain I'm just built differently than she is. I have to take a drink and count to ten before I continue.

Before I can say another word, Cristiano sits up and leans forward as he addresses my mom, "We've talked about this. I understand your concerns. Even though I thought maybe I might have children someday, I'm willing to take Jordan's lead on this issue. I love this woman for who she is, and if she doesn't want to have children, I can't separate it out. Either I love none of her or I love all of her — there is no in between."

"Still, don't you think you might resent it later?"

"I went into this relationship with my eyes wide open. It would be unfair of me to resent her later for how she feels," Cristiano asserts.

I scoot closer to Cristiano and melt into his side as I absorb his support. Although he's speaking to my mother, I wonder if he is also trying to convey a message to me. If he is, his message is received. Despite his assurances to the contrary, part of me always worries Cristiano doesn't completely understand where I'm coming from and is just going along to get along without really supporting the choices I've made. His comments to my family and his sister make it clear he does get it. Not only does he get it, but he also loves me in spite of my unusual choice.

My mom studies both of us carefully before she says, "Jordie, I don't mean to be hard on you, honey. You're asking this man to give up his family legacy and I want to know for sure he agrees. I don't want you to be like Jaxson."

Jaxson looks a little stunned that the focus of the conversation has turned to him. "What do you mean, Mom?"

"Well, we all know Marquette wasn't who she pretended to be. Your child lost her life because of Marquette's lies," my mom responds in a bitter tone.

Jaxson sighs as he drags his hand down his face. Donda reaches out to grab his free hand. I can see her willing strength into my brother. I watch as he takes a calming breath before he says, "Jasmine died because Marquette was addicted to drugs and didn't seek help. I will forever live with the guilt that I didn't know what was going on sooner. I can't change the past. I can only build a future together with Donda."

"All I was saying was —" my mom starts.

This is not a fight Jaxson should have to be involved in. I try a different tactic. "Mom, look at me. I mean, really look at me. Look how I'm dressed. Specifically, look at what I'm not wearing."

After a moment, my mom says, "You are not wearing body makeup."

"Exactly!" I exclaim. "Cristiano took a leap of faith

and believed in me when no one else did. He helped me start a whole new venture in the fashion business. His support and the life stories of my clients have given me the courage to show the world who I really am. My life has changed dramatically since I met Cristiano. He has made it clear he is in my corner regardless of what I choose to do. Do you have any idea how that makes me feel?"

My mom looks wistful. "I do actually. I had someone who believed in me like that once. I wish I had been brave enough to hold onto him and not let other people change my mind."

"So you understand. As cliché as it is, Cristiano feels like the other half of me — he's the missing part. Mom, please stop trying to talk him out of being with me. I made my decision. I love him and plan to be in this relationship for as long as he'll have me."

A tear slides down my mom's face. "Okay. I'll try to relax and enjoy the fact that my baby daughter is in love with a kind and gentle man."

I get up and give my mom a hug as I admit, "It'll be okay Mom. Believe me, no one is more surprised than I am that Cristiano loves me."

⎯⎯◆●⎯⎯

As Cristiano and I sit in front of the roaring fireplace in his hotel room, he rubs my neck to help relieve the tension. "This will seem like a dumb question, but is your mom always like that or was there something about me which upsets her?"

I shrug. "The relationship between us has never

been easy — but after Jasmine died, the strain between us became overwhelming. My mom was more than willing to forgive Marquette for what she did. It took me years to even ponder the idea. I was so angry and hurt. I was nearly impossible to deal with in those days. I was pissed off at everyone, including God. I couldn't understand why something so horrendous could happen to such a sweet little soul. To be honest, I still don't understand."

"Today's dinner did not go as I expected. I thought your mom would be giving me the third degree, not you."

"Why would she be hard on you? She doesn't know you." I roll my neck to loosen my tight muscles.

"At one point in my life, I was the kind of boy mothers warned their girls against dating. If your mom is Internet savvy, she's probably run across a few media accounts of the way I once was. To say my late teens and early twenties weren't pretty is an understatement."

"I think that's part of the reason my mother doesn't exactly trust me to make good decisions on my own. My story isn't much different from yours. She's disappointed I didn't turn into a younger version of her. I had more than a few 'bees in my bonnet' as my mother would say. It took me a while to figure out who I was and what I stood for."

Cristiano leans over and kisses me thoroughly before he says, "I wouldn't worry about it. I think it's a rite of passage for parents to be disappointed with their children. The good news is you came out of that experience as a strong, vibrant, compassionate human being. As far as I'm concerned, no parent could ask for more than the type of woman you are. I am proud to be your boyfriend."

I reach up and pull him closer as I return his kiss.

"This isn't a place I expected to find myself in, but I'm so glad to be here." I place my ear against his chest as I revel in the comfort of his steady heartbeat. As difficult as today's dinner was, it reinforced the fact that Cristiano loves me for me. Despite all the obstacles we face, the thought is enough to make my heart happy.

"I think we should celebrate that we survived the Shepherd inquisition," I declare as I stand up and hold out my hand toward him. When he gives me his hand, I kiss his knuckles and then walk toward the bed.

"Far be it from me to stand in the way of a good plan."

My breathing becomes slow and shallow as he worships my body with his eyes. Yes, being in love is worth all the risk. Who says there's only one path to love?

CHAPTER TWENTY

CRISTIANO

NERVOUSLY, I STRAIGHTEN MY tie and look over at Jordan. She is trying to buckle her shoe, and she's not paying any attention to my fidgeting.

"Do I look like a competent adult?" I ask when she looks up.

She laughs softly as she walks over and fixes my tie and adds a tie clip. "There, that's better — but you always appear like a competent adult. Even when you're messing around on four wheelers and covered in mud."

Jordan smells so phenomenal I forget what we are talking about for a second. Struggling to focus, I say, "I was a little surprised when your brother gave me the all-clear to ride four wheelers with him. I expected him to be much more conservative."

Jordan brushes my shoulder with her fingertips. "It's been almost six months since your shoulder surgery, and Jaxson is thrilled with how your physical therapy is going. Jaxson would not give his okay to an activity which might injure you."

I roll my eyes. "I had to bite my tongue pretty hard that day to keep from telling your brother the 'challenging hills' he was taking me on were similar to the ones I mastered when I was eight years old."

She snickers as her eyes light up. "It probably was best you kept that thought to yourself. My brother and I are very competitive. If you had said something like that, Jaxson would've worked hard to prove you wrong."

"Really? He seems like such a laid-back kind of guy."

Jordan shakes her head. "My brother has you totally fooled. Who do you think taught me to play basketball? We used to scrimmage all the time, and we would play until we almost passed out."

"It's too bad your brother is a doctor and not a lawyer. I think I could use some competitive help today. I don't know why Rowden has called such an official meeting with the attorney. I hope he's not planning to sue me."

"If he does, you can join the 'pending litigation club' with me. Maybe CJ will give us a volume discount," Jordan responds with a playful smirk.

"You can joke all you want, but I'm a little freaked out. The last time we had lawyers involved in a conversation between us it was to set up our partnership so we could produce our podcast. It's been years." I re-tuck my shirt.

"Cristiano, try to breathe. You haven't done anything wrong. You just had a disagreement with Rowden over creative differences. You didn't take it to the media or anyplace public, and I haven't said a word to anyone. I have a hard time believing someone who has been your friend for so long would take any legal action over something so small."

I bow my head in frustration. "Yeah I know. It's hard not to notice a lot of strange things have been happening to us recently. People are weird. Like I said, Rowden and Jubilee have been acting oddly lately."

Jordan stands on her tiptoes before she brushes a soft kiss on my lips, "No matter what happens, you will always be my hero. You gave me a chance when it looked like my luck had run out. I'm sure everything will be fine. I'll be in a meeting with a client, but text me when you know what's going on, please."

I pull her into a tight embrace before I whisper in her ear, "Thanks for the pep talk. I really needed it. I love you more than you could know."

⸺●⸺

The ticking clock sounds like cannons at a football game. With every heartbeat, it feels as if the walls close in a little more. To kill time, I try to start a casual conversation, "How are you doing?"

My heart sinks when Rowden replies, "I think that's something our lawyer should answer for you. He'll be here in a moment. He was just waylaid by a phone call."

Exasperated, I try to get more information from his wife. "Jubilee, what happened? How did our relationship disintegrate to the point where we need to speak through lawyers? I used to come over to your house every weekend and barbecue. You were like a second mother to me during those years."

Jubilee blanches white and then picks up a tissue and dabs at her eyes. "The lawyer will explain everything, I promise."

Jubilee's solemn words chill me to my bones. By the time the attorney finally comes in the room, I feel like I'm going to throw up.

As soon as he sits down, I ask, "Now can someone tell me why I'm here?"

The lawyer holds out his hand for me to shake. "Wesley Wydell, it's a pleasure to meet you."

After I shake his hand, I comment, "Wish I could say the same. My history with the justice system has been fascinating, but a little less than fun."

"I'm sorry Mr. Romero, it was never the Randalls' intent to upset you. They were hoping this would be the easiest forum for them to keep you abreast of what's happening."

I look over at Rowden and narrow my gaze. "A phone call wouldn't work?"

"Not for this, Cris," Jubilee responds softly.

I address Mr. Wydell in a clipped voice. "Help me understand."

The lawyer consults his paperwork as he says, "Mr. Randall acknowledges you were the key architect of *Xyresic*. The show's content, structure and format are your intellectual property."

I turn back to Rowden abruptly as I ask, "Are you suing me for something?"

"Oh for Pete's sake, Wesley, spit it out. Don't use your big lawyer words. Speak regular English like the rest of us," Jubilee says.

I swallow hard as I wait for the attorney to speak.

The attorney nods at Jubilee. "Very well then. Jubilee and Rowden brought you here today to tell you they are relinquishing any rights to the show you developed."

"What? Why? I thought you said we were on the verge of a deal with ESPN," I sputter.

"All that is true, but, Jubilee and I have discovered some things are more important than chasing the almighty dollar. Jubs has been diagnosed with ALS. No one knows exactly how long she'll live. She has enough things to fill up three or four bucket lists. She might not even have the chance to get through one."

"No!" I whisper harshly.

Jubilee and Rowden nod, their pain is spelled out clearly on their faces. Rowden takes a gulp of coffee. "So, this show was your idea, your concept, and your talent. It only stands to reason the show should be yours."

I'm still trying to wrap my brain around the fact that Jubilee is sick. She doesn't look ill yet. I saw her stumble the other day, but I thought it was because she and Rowden had drinks over lunch. I didn't even consider the possibility it could be related to something long-term or serious. I'm struggling to absorb the devastating news I wasn't exaggerating when I said Jubilee is like a second mother to me.

"At least let me buy you out," I blurt. "You were my partner in this business if you hadn't given me the encouragement to start and the financing to make it happen, there would be no show."

"That's what I told them, but they wouldn't listen," mutters the attorney. "They have elected to disregard my advice and proceed on their own path."

"Money is not the issue. When you and I split, you won't find an executive director who will work for peanuts like I did. You'll need more loot to hire a good ED."

"Won't you need the money for medical bills?"

"The minute I set foot on a racetrack, Jubilee insisted we get as much insurance coverage as we possibly could. She was deathly afraid I would go off and do something stupid like crash and break my neck."

I glance over at Jubilee in surprise. "You guys are two of the most careful riders I've seen, inside the circuit or out. Even so, I'm glad you have enough insurance."

"Yeah, the premiums were killer, but my paranoia paid off," Jubilee says with a tearful smile.

In the face of such a devastating diagnosis, it's almost impossible to focus on business. Still, that's why we're here, so I plunge forward. "When does this new agreement go into effect?"

"Jubilee would like to go on a road trip in a couple weeks. She wants to go see Mount Rushmore and stuff like that while she's still strong enough to make the trip."

"Do the execs at ESPN know about this?"

"Not yet, we wanted to tell you first," Jubilee responds. "But I have a feeling they are going to be thrilled." She looks over at Rowden. "My husband loves me more than life itself, but sometimes he makes stupid decisions because he thinks it might make me happy. One of those decisions was the new direction he wanted to take your show. I mentioned to Rowden that watching reality shows like the *Real Housewives* or *The Kardashians* took my mind off my health. Somehow in his generous mind, he turned it around to mean I was asking him to make your sports coverage more like modern reality television. Just like with the Scrabble word, I never wanted him to make changes to your show. I simply wanted him to acknowledge the things I like. Sometimes he gets a little focused on the sports world and forgets everything else."

"I'm so sorry you're facing these challenges," I offer. "But I take it you wouldn't object if I changed the name of the show?"

Jubilee shakes her head as she replies, "No, it's your turn now. Do whatever you want with it. Just a suggestion — I think the name should be changed to something people can actually pronounce and remember."

"Do you still feel well enough to do some design work for me?" I ask as I study her movements.

Jubilee cringes but nods. "I can still work on the computer. Sometimes I'm a little slower than I used to be, but I get the job done."

"Rowden, I am going to change the name of the show, but I'll have Jubilee draw up the graphics. That way, the show remains the tribute to Jubilee you always hoped it would be."

"Thank you, Cris. I don't even know what to say. I am touched by your generosity."

"I'm not the one who is being overwhelmingly

generous here. You guys are. I will do my best to stay true to our partnership and make the show everything we dreamed it would be. You two go on and enjoy your retirement."

"We appreciate that. We really do. Tell me, if I get frustrated with having Rowden around all the time, can I kick him back into the studio to do some work for you? Sometimes he gets underfoot, and it drives me crazy."

I smile at Jubilee as I stand up, walk around the table and hug her from behind. "Consider this a standing invitation for you to come back and participate in the show. After all, without you, there wouldn't have been a show. I owe you guys more thanks than I can express."

"No son, we owe you. It's been your talent and insight over the years which brought the fans in. Your sports analysis and commentary are some of the best out there. It's been a privilege, but now I have to go take care of my wife."

"You do that. When I marry Jordan, you will be the first people on my guest list."

"You've proposed to the lovely young girl who designed your clothes?" Jubilee asks as she grins from ear to ear. She hops up from her chair and runs over to give me a hug.

"I got a little ahead of myself. I'm trying to be patient and let all of her legal problems and the rehab from my surgery play out, but I'm losing patience. As you know, I never did have a lot of patience to spare."

Rowden watches Jubilee return to her chair with sad eyes. "If you have found love in your life, grab onto it with both hands. You never know when the thing you love the most might be taken away. It's the worst feeling ever."

"Rowden, I'm not dead. Don't put me in the grave just yet."

Rowden looks over at Jubilee, his expression full of anxiety. "I know Jubilee, but the very thought of losing you makes me wake up in a cold sweat."

"You can't think that way. Scientists are working on new cures every day. Maybe, I'll be one of the pioneers in the new treatment methods, and it won't be as devastating as it is right now," Jubilee says as she strokes her husband's arm.

"I hope that's exactly what happens. You are strong and have a great attitude. I can't thank the two of you enough for all you've done for me. I will try to make your legacy last."

Rowden's voice is thick with unshed tears as he responds, "I appreciate it. Jubilee and I want you to know we think the world of you. We know you'll make your new show a smashing success."

"I'll sure try."

The lawyer clears his throat. "Do you want to sign all the paperwork today or do you want to postpone it until you've gotten over the shock of the announcement?"

"Just give me a few minutes to collect myself and then I'll sign. It sounds like Rowden and Jubilee need to go on vacation as soon as they can. I don't want to bog down the process."

The lawyer looks at his watch. "I'm free at one

thirty if you want to come back later."

I sag against the side of the building as I pull my phone out to contact Jordan. My hands are shaking from the adrenaline coursing through my body. This has been an incredibly confusing day. I am heartbroken that Jubilee is sick. Yet, I now have the opportunity able to save my show the way I intended. I'm not sure how to reconcile those two concepts.

I text Jordan in case she is still in the meeting with her client, but she calls me back immediately and demands, "Don't keep me in suspense! What happened? Are they going to sue you?"

"We assumed all the wrong things, and now I feel terrible for doubting my friends. It was surreal."

"Is everything all right?" Jordan asks. Even through the phone, I can feel her compassion.

"Well, for starters Jubilee is sick with ALS. So, Rowden wants to take her on a vacation to tackle some of the things she had on her bucket list. Apparently, her list is quite long and she's getting weaker by the day. You won't believe this, but Rowden and Jubilee turned the business over to me — lock stock and barrel. I can do anything I want with it now."

"That's grea —" Jordan starts before trailing off. "I don't know what to think about this. I was hoping for a huge breakthrough in your career, but I didn't mean for it to come this way."

"I didn't either. Now I've got to sign paperwork to make it all official." I laugh wryly. "I went into this meeting thinking I would be sued or kicked to the curb. In my wildest dreams, I never thought they'd turn over the whole show to me."

"Are you worried about what all this means for your show?" Jordan asks.

I sigh. "I probably should be. Honestly, the first thought which occurred to me was that I can finally reside in the same city as you and live a little less out of my suitcase."

"You know I would love that. I'm so sorry all this is happening. But, it might be like you say, in all the darkness you have to find your own silver lining."

"When did I say that?" I ask as I rest my head against the building and struggle not to cry.

"You said it right after I thought my life was completely ruined and my career blown up into smithereens."

"Well, I guess I should be smart and listen to myself. That sounds like good advice," I draw in a deep breath. "I'll be home after I get all this done. Bear with me because I don't think I feel like celebrating even though this should be a happy day."

Jordan clicks her tongue at me. "Of course not. No one would ever expect you to celebrate the fact that your friend is sick — even if it means good news for you."

"Thanks, Jordan. I … I should probably go."

"Give me a call later, if you need to talk," Jordan says. "Or even if you don't."

Once again, I am in awe of Jordan's generosity and how well she knows me. In my eyes, she is just about perfect.

CHAPTER TWENTY-ONE

JORDAN

I watch as Cristiano packs his bags yet again. "I thought you'd be traveling less after you moved to Oregon."

"The X-Games are in Aspen this year. It's further for me to travel at the moment."

"So, why am I not moving to Colorado?" I retrieve his shaving kit from the bathroom.

Cristiano puts down his socks and walks over to me. He envelops me in a hug. "I know this is rough, but I hope I'll be able to add more reporters to my show and spread out the workload."

"You would leave the field? I thought the interviews were your favorite part of your job."

"I do love it — but I love you more. If I have to cut back on my interaction with the racing world to help our relationship, it is a sacrifice I'm willing to make."

I cringe at his use of the word sacrifice. "I wish there was an easier way to balance all of this. I hate to see you cut back on what you enjoy. I don't want you to learn to hate your job. I've been there — it's not fun."

He places his hands on my shoulders, "Don't worry about it, this frantic stage is temporary. Once I get settled into a rhythm, I'll be able to manage my assignments better."

"Has Scott agreed to come on as your Executive Director?" I rest my cheek on Cristiano's chest.

"Oh, I forgot to tell you. Scott will be officially on board next month. He has to finish up the assignment he's on, and then he'll be on team Romero."

"That should make your life a little easier, right?"

"That's my hope," Cristiano gives me a quick peck on the cheek. "I'm sorry. I wish I could stay, but I don't want to be late for boarding."

I pull his face down and kiss him deeply. "I'll be here when you get back," I murmur in his ear as I pull away.

"I'm counting on it," Cristiano admits as he runs his thumb over my bottom lip. "I'll call you when I get back to Aspen."

"Make it a video call, and I'll show you some new things I've designed for myself," I reply with a wink.

Cristiano groans. "That was just mean."

I smile slyly. "I think I warned you in advance that I have more than a little mean in me."

As we walk out the door, Cristiano slaps me on the backside and says, "You know what they say about payback …"

As I walk downstairs to refill my coffee cup, Donda is standing at the sink looking out the window. She looks lost in thought and jumps as I cough discreetly.

"Are you all right?"

Donda wipes away a tear as she answers, "Yeah, I'm fine. I'm just watching Gabriel play with Kennadie in the yard. I can't believe how close I came to losing it all because of bad decisions I made when I was young. My babies could have been motherless."

"Jaxson caught your symptoms early. If there's anything I've learned in my life, it's you can't go back and second-guess your past. You can't change it, you can only move forward."

She sighs softly. "I know you're right. Still, a part of me can't help but feel guilty. What if the worst would've happened?"

"Then my brother would've stepped up and been even more of an amazing father. I thought Jaxson said everything was on track with your recovery," I ask with alarm.

"As far as anyone can tell, the valve repair went off without a hitch, but it still was terrifying. Listen to me going on and on about myself. How are you? I hear your sewing machine going nearly twenty-four hours a day. Don't you ever take a break?"

I shrug. "I don't have much else to do when Cristiano is not around. So, I figure I should try to get as much of my collection done as possible so when he's here, I can spend time with him."

"How is that going? Have you decided whether you're going to rent some space for JS Couture?"

"I don't really know yet. A lot of it depends on what Cristiano decides to do. He doesn't feel right staying here with me, but he hasn't found a place yet either. He's been living out of one of those extended-stay hotels. I know he'd love to have a real home."

"So why don't you guys get a house? I am sure you'd like your privacy back. Not to mention that I'm sure there are perks to actually seeing your boyfriend —" Donda says with a comical, exaggerated wink.

I snicker at her expression. I can't say she's wrong though. "You make a compelling argument. Maybe I'll bring it up the next time he's in town. I hate the thought of putting any more stress on him."

"If you guys are anything like Jaxson and me, things got easier once we settled the whole living arrangements thing."

This time, I laugh out loud, "Settle you did. You guys made a baby. That's not our goal. I just want to see my boyfriend every once in a while when he is happy, healthy and not sick from eating takeout food."

Donda scoffs at me. "You know what causes babies, right? Or, does your brother need to have another talk with you?"

I hide my head in my hands. "Oh please tell me he did not tell you that story."

"I'll never tell," vows Donda. "But, just so you know, Gabriel's reaction to the same talk was equally squeamish."

"All I can say is don't have your big brother whose wife just had a baby tell you about the facts of life. It will scar you forever," I respond with a shudder as I remember our lengthy, detailed conversation.

"I can tell you for a fact that Jaxson's descriptions probably weren't candid enough."

"Well, not everyone delivers their baby in the car on the way to the hospital," I quip.

"Come to think of it, it's probably a good thing I was brutally honest with Gabriel because he was front and center when Kennadie was born."

"You are so bad! Poor Gabriel is going to be compulsive about using birth control now."

"I can only hope there were some upsides to my unscheduled delivery."

"Did my brother know how devious you are when you guys fell in love?"

"Since Gabriel was the one to play matchmaker, he probably expected much worse. Gabriel didn't keep any secrets to himself."

"That sounds like my mom, she was airing all sorts of dirty laundry when she met Cristiano. It's a wonder he didn't go screaming through the streets."

"Nonsense. That man thinks the sun rises and sets at your command."

A sense of contentment settles in my heart as I answer, "I agree. I still pinch myself every day. I am afraid if I blink, it will all go away."

Donda glances out the window at Kennadie and Gabriel playing in the yard. "I understand. Trust me, I'm right there with you."

Brando is barking his little heart out. I hear the doorbell ring, but I am in the middle of doing box pleats. There is a certain rhythm to forming them, and I don't want to stop to answer the door. It's probably one of Gabriel's friends, anyway. He can grab the door. Keeping one ear trained on the sounds downstairs, I continue to sew.

I practically jump out of my seat when my phone starts to vibrate. Reluctantly, I stop and check my messages. It might be Cristiano. The weather is dicey where he's at, and he wasn't sure if his flight would take off.

To my surprise, it's from Gabriel. He says I have a guest. I sigh as I look down at my yoga pants and stretched out T-shirt. Of course, I couldn't have company yesterday when I decided to dress up and send Cristiano a video message.

I gather up the fabric in my lap and gently place it on the cutting board beside me. My heart skips a beat when I consider the possibility Cristiano may have changed his tickets to fly out earlier because of the weather. I practically run down the stairs and throw open the door.

When I see who it is, I gasp. Aisha laughs when she sees my expression. "I take it I'm not the person you hoped to see."

"No, but … it's awesome to see you. Come on in. Excuse the way I'm dressed. I wasn't expecting guests. I'm working on a very complicated garment right now."

"Don't apologize. I'm the one who stopped by without an appointment. I couldn't wait to share the news."

"What news?" I ask, bewildered. I haven't spoken to Aisha since I finished her last custom order a few months ago.

"Oh, I guess you're probably a little behind. Wow! You might want to sit down for this."

I flinch. "Is it bad? Am I going to need something stronger than a cup of tea?"

"I think you'll want champagne after you hear what I have to say," Aisha answers with a huge grin.

"Don't tease me like that." I scoot forward on the couch. Trying not to show my nerves, I hold a throw pillow on my lap. My heart is racing, and I don't even know why.

"Well ... you know how much I love the stuff you designed for me?" Aisha says as her eyes flash with excitement. "I may have told a few dozen, or a couple hundred people about what you're doing with your design studio."

I swallow hard. Outside of the interview we did to counter Mishka's accusations and the red-carpet event I attended with Cristiano, I haven't done much to promote my brand. I've been too busy fulfilling custom orders for a variety of people.

I finally find my voice as I say, "Wow, Aisha. I'm glad you liked your stuff, but I didn't expect you to act like my one-person PR team. That's just too much."

Aisha digs a piece of paper out of her purse and

hands it to me. "No, it's not. I'm glad I had a chance to do it. I feel responsible for finding you this opportunity."

I open the piece of paper and try to make sense of the email I'm reading. "What is this?" I ask.

"After you did such a good job for me, I started spreading the news to all of my friends who are in the media. Many of them run fashion blogs or have segments on their local news. I put together a video package of all the designs you've done. People were incredibly touched by your mission. One of the companies who took the most interest is a mobility company called Movement and a Half."

I looked at her blankly as I say, "I've never heard of them."

"Most people haven't. It's a husband and wife team who own a company which distributes specialized wheelchairs — you know, the ones they play basketball in?"

"I knew a guy in college who used one of those."

"Anyway, the husband contacted me. At first, he wanted to know if you might be able to make his wife some clothes which don't get caught in the wheels of her chair. We started corresponding back and forth about other outfits you've made for individuals with disabilities. Matthew and Kalina came up with the idea of expanding their product line to include clothes."

I place the pillow I'm holding behind my back and lean against it "How would they go from selling wheelchairs to selling clothes? I can't sew any faster. I don't even have a space for my shop yet — even if I could afford to hire someone," I stammer.

"Slow down. Before you talk yourself out of the idea, I think you should speak to Matthew and Kalina. They seem pretty innovative. Besides, you don't have any solid plans for your business, right? What could it hurt to speak with them?"

"I don't know. It probably wouldn't hurt to talk to them. It's a lot to wrap my brain around."

"I guess you better buckle in because I'm not done," Aisha announces.

"There's more?"

"Have you heard from your attorney recently?" Aisha asks.

"No, her office said she would be out of town. I guess she had a family emergency of some sort."

"Listen, I'm good friends with a reporter who covers the court beat. He heard from a source of his that Mishka has filed paperwork to drop the case against you."

"What? Are you sure this source is reliable? They could be yanking my chain. I wouldn't put it past Mishka to try to do something like this to throw me off." I am trying to remain calm, but inside, I feel like I'm gasping for air. This may be the break I was praying for.

Aisha shrugs. "I don't think that's what this is. When I first met you and heard the accusations against you, I had the investigators from our news station look into Mishka, they found the same sort of damaging information."

"Information?" My heart beats out of my chest.

"Yeah, I guess since your story came out on Madison's show, people started coming forward.

Apparently, you're not the first design graduate to intern for Mishka. How old did she say she was?" Aisha asks me.

I shrug as I say, "I don't know — probably in her early forties, why?"

"It turns out Mishka Silk is actually closer to fifty. You are not the first intern she has used to build her career. Before she was Mishka Silk, she was Cashmere Cottonwood and before that she was Elouise Hadley. Two former interns have come forward to tell their story. It seems Ms. Silk doesn't want the world to know she has multiple identities. These women's stories are remarkably similar to yours. Apparently, she promised to make them stars in the fashion industry, but never let them actually work as official designers. One of them has been providing garments to Mishka for years."

I frown. "I know that story all too well. So, how did she react when the other two interns left? Did Mishka sue them too?"

"Not specifically. But she threatened to ruin one intern's shot at a scholarship, and she threatened to blackball the other. It appears you are the only person she actually filed a lawsuit against."

"Interesting," I comment.

"The first intern provided documentation of her conversations with Mishka to the school, so they didn't listen to Mishka's complaints. The second woman moved out of the country when her military husband was stationed overseas, so Mishka didn't bother to mess with her. She just trashed her reputation locally."

"Oh joy. I wonder why she decided to sue me and

not the others?"

Aisha leans forward and talks to me softly, "Okay, this is completely off the record. I don't want to ruin my source — but apparently, she told some court personnel the reason she went after you was because she figured you wouldn't fight back. She was banking that you would be too embarrassed about your vitiligo to appear publicly."

Something about that strikes me as funny, and I laugh, "Really? She used to shove me in front of the camera all the time. It was like an obsession with her. She always tried to catch me off guard and looking terrible. I always figured it was her strategy to look better and more put together than I was. I learned to dress to the nines every time I went to work. I never knew when she would make me appear on her behalf. So, for her to say I was too camera shy to respond to her complaints is a bit disingenuous at best. At most, it was a rash strategic decision."

Aisha rolls her eyes. "Anybody who watches the television interviews with her can tell she is a few cards shy of a full deck. I wouldn't worry about it. Even if she did take this to court, I think you would have easily won — even without the testimony of the other two women. Either way, without someone else providing the designs for her, her empire will crumble."

My hands tremble as I run them through my hair. "That's true. You can't run a design business unless you can produce products. After the way she's been treating me, I can't say I am sad it's all crashing down at her feet. If she was stealing another artist's designs, she doesn't deserve any respect."

"I absolutely agree. I think you should put this all behind you and meet with Matt and Kalina. It's time for you to stop being in a holding pattern and move forward with JS Couture."

"At some point, I probably will. But it's going to take a few days for all of this to sink in. There are so many decisions to make and things to verify. My brain is spinning a million miles a minute."

"When you make it big, just remember you were once a peon like the rest of us."

"Oh, don't be modest. I saw you on the red carpet talking to huge stars. Don't try to pretend you're a nobody. I know better. You are a kick-butt reporter. A bigger market is a given. Someday soon, some smart head honcho will snatch you up, and you won't be able to take the time to drop by Oregon just to say hi."

"You know I will always be a fan. Anyway, I think what you're doing with your business is beyond phenomenal. I'll support it any way I can."

"Thank you so much, Aisha. I'm glad I could turn you into a fan. Somewhere along the process, you've become my friend too."

Aisha winks at me. "Take your time absorbing all of this." A chime sounds on Aisha's phone. When she picks it up and sees the time, she says, "I need to go. If I don't, I'll be late for my cousin's rehearsal dinner. Good luck explaining this to Cristiano."

I nod at Aisha. "I can't thank you enough for advocating for my business."

"Any time," Aisha stands up to leave.

When I open the door for her, I reach out and give her a hug. "I'm grateful I was able to make friends like you on this journey. Although it royally sucked to leave Mishka, I think it was the best thing that's ever happened to me."

"Not a problem, but be sure to tell me what you decide." Her phone beeps again. She scowls at it and then says, "I have to go. Call me. Promise?"

"I will. I promise," I say with a crooked smile.

As I shut the door behind her, I lean against it and sob. Is it possible all of this is over and I can move on with my life?

Almost without thinking, I dial Cristiano's number and wait for his face to appear on the video call. After I dial, I remember he might be on an airplane. I guess if he is, the call will go through to his voicemail.

I'm surprised when I see him on the other end of the phone. He takes one look at my red nose and watery eyes and asks, "What's wrong? Is it Donda or Kennadie?"

"No, they are fine. This time, it's about us."

CHAPTER TWENTY-TWO

CRISTIANO

THE FLIGHT ATTENDANT IS giving me the stink eye as I examine my phone closely. I can't figure out what's going on with Jordan. My heart pounds with fear. I'm not sure what happened, but she looks incredibly torn up. When I called her earlier in the day to tell her about the weather, everything seemed normal. As her picture disappears from my phone, I wonder if maybe she's discovered my secret and is horrified by what I've done. Her parting words sounded ominous.

I sink back into my chair as I try to find space for my legs. I swear, every time I get on a plane, the leg room gets smaller. These days, you practically have to be a child to be comfortable on a plane. Fortunately, this is a pretty short flight.

I can't wait to get home and talk to Jordan face-to-face. Video calls are cool, but they're still not enough. I've been gone for what seems like forever this time — longer than I expected. I had to add some meetings with the executives at ESPN because of the change in my programming. I've decided to name the new version of the show, *The X-Games: Razor's Edge* in homage to Rowden and Jubilee. Scott and I have elected to focus on the races while giving our viewers time to get to know each athlete a little better. Not salacious, tabloid garbage — rather we'll focus how they grew up and entered the world of competition. Scott has seen this approach work before when he worked on the Olympic Games and he's used to putting those kinds of packages together. I am excited about the new reincarnation of my business. It's much more in line with what I envisioned when I first started.

I think Scott and I will work well as a team. He seems excited to be on the project, and I'm lucky to have him. When I told Jubilee about the new title and direction of the show, she was thrilled. It turns out that the little personal vignettes about athletes are her favorite part of the Olympics.

Jubilee was totally on board when I asked her to design our new title graphics and materials for advertising. Apparently, the doctors have her on a new trial medication and it's showing promise. That drug trial is so secretive, even Jubilee doesn't know the name of the medication. She told me she didn't care what it was called as long as it works. Jubilee reports she's feeling stronger than she has in a long time. Rowden sounds much better now as well. It is the most hopeful I've seen him since I learned about Jubilee's diagnosis. Apparently, Rowden and Jubilee had a wonderful vacation to Mount Rushmore, and they are happily settling into retirement.

Before Jordan's odd phone call, I was eagerly anticipating revealing the second phase of my move to

Oregon. I have been keeping this secret for a while. I was waiting for things to resolve with Rowden and Jubilee, but now that they have, I can move forward. The timing couldn't be more perfect. The Potter family was motivated to sell because they needed the money to build a mother-in-law cottage onto their kid's home. So, I was able to purchase my portion of the American dream for a steal.

Now, I have to go home and see what's wrong with Jordan before I show her what I've done.

———————◆———————

I don't even get all the way to the front porch before Jordan comes running out of the house and throws herself into my arms. I have to drop my carry-on bag so I can catch her. She rains kisses all over my face and hugs me tight. "You'll never believe this!"

"Believe what?" I set her down and grab my suitcase. Placing my arm around her waist, we walk up the porch steps together and go in the house.

She pulls me over to the couch. "Okay, this story will be a little confusing, but I have to tell you what happened while you were away."

I relax a little when I realize she doesn't seem to be in tears anymore. She looks more like a kid who is waiting to open presents on Christmas morning.

"Well, you remember Aisha, the reporter who interviewed us on the red carpet? You know, the one from *Are You Really Gonna Wear That?!* —"

"Sure. She's been referring a ton of clients to you, right?"

"Yes, I have made a bunch of clothes for her now. Aisha is more like a friend from college than a client. Anyway, she stopped by the house today. Aisha had big news for me."

"Don't leave me in suspense. I want to know why you look like you just won the lottery."

"In a way I did. I won a game I didn't even realize I was playing."

"I'm sorry, I must be jet-lagged. I don't understand. What exactly happened?" I try to follow the conversation.

"It turns out Aisha is not just a fan of my work, but she's been working unofficially as my PR person. She is well-connected in the fashion industry and was publicizing my stuff on her blog and in private meetings with different people in the industry. Apparently, she made a little promo video of my work and what JS Couture stands for."

"That's epically cool of her. I bet you feel good."

"Oh, I can't even tell you. You could have knocked me over with a feather when she told me all this. You know what makes me feel even better than the video? The offer from a company which provides mobility equipment. They want me to design a line of adaptive clothing they can offer in their stores and on their website. I don't know much about this company, but their website seems well put together, and they look very professional."

"Have you been able to speak with them yet?"

"By the time I was done talking to Aisha, their offices were closed. I left a voicemail — so they should call me back tomorrow."

"But, you've seen their offer?" I press.

"I saw the email they sent Aisha. They definitely seem interested. Obviously, there were no specific figures or anything. It seemed legit."

As Jordan provides me with more details, I begin to share her optimism. "I can see why you're so excited. This is an enormous opportunity for you." Jordan gets up to pace and I stand up and pull her into a loose embrace. "I am so proud of you."

Jordan grins even wider. "You would think that would be enough life-changing news for a single day, right?"

"Well, it is pretty big news," I admit.

"That's what I thought too — but it wasn't even the most extraordinary news I received today."

"It isn't?" I enjoy the sparkle in Jordan's eyes. I haven't seen her look this happy in months. "What could possibly be better than a potential contract to help you launch your business?"

"What if I told you the cloud which has been hanging over my head almost since the day we met is gone?"

"Mishka? What happened to her?"

"Nothing happened to her exactly — except her house of lies has begun to crumble."

My smile grows wider with every word. "Tell me more." I grip Jordan's hands, eager to hear the details.

"This is where it gets weird. Most of this, I didn't

even know. Come to think of it, I didn't know any of it. It turns out Mishka is much older than she told me she was and I am not the first eager design student she's taken advantage of. Two more women came forward to say they had similar experiences to mine. While I was working for her and handling the business end of things, she had another student who was creating her work."

"Wow! That takes some *cojones*. I'm amazed she wasn't caught before now."

"Frankly, I am too. It does explain a lot of things. When I was arranging her social schedule, I tried to get her to do some television appearances where she would talk about her design process, but every time one of those bookings got close, she would come up with some reason to cancel the appearance."

"Apparently, Mishka didn't know much about design at all." I smirk. "What does this mean for you?"

"It means Mishka doesn't want all of this to come out in court because it would expose her as a fraud. So, she has dropped the lawsuit against me. I am finally free to move on with my life. I can plan a future for my business."

"That is great news. I am so happy for you. Now you can put the past behind you and go forward."

"I can't tell you how phenomenal this feels. I didn't realize how scared I was living until I don't have to feel that way anymore."

"I'm sorry she put you through all that when she was the one who is living a lie. It was wrong. I wonder what CJ will have to say about it? Given all the crazy things she's said in the past about us. I don't know if it's a good idea to drop our defamation suit. But, CJ will be able to tell you more."

The light in Jordan's eyes dims. "I suppose you're right. Even so, I would just as soon not have to mess with all the legal stuff anymore."

"I understand how you feel, Jor — but someone has to hold Mishka Silk accountable for her behavior."

Jordan sighs. "I was kinda hoping good old karma would do the trick. Still, I hear what you're saying. I'll talk to CJ."

I try to keep my voice under control as I address her so I don't give away my whole secret. "Aisha is not the only person who has news today. Are you ready for another surprise?"

"If the surprise has anything to do with dinner, I'm all over it. I'm starving." As if to underscore the point, Jordan's stomach lets out a huge growl.

I pull her up to her feet and go to the sideboard to get her purse. "Dinner can be arranged, if we hurry."

⬥

As soon as we reach the car, Jordan breaks into a fit of laughter. She tucks herself into the passenger seat and puts the to-go container on her lap.

"Cristiano, I love you, but I think you scarred the server for life. Your Latin charm is a little too much — especially when you turn it up to high gear."

"What? All I did was ask for some pie to go."

"The way you were caressing the banana cream pie with your eyes made it seem like you have very naughty plans later," Jordan spits out with a gust of laughter. "Then, you insisted she deliver it to you as quickly as possible. Who knows what's going through the woman's mind? She was giving me the side eye. I couldn't tell if she was angry at me for being with you or she was just jealous I'm so lucky."

I chuckle as I respond, "Okay, two things. First, there's nothing to say I don't have naughty plans for later. Second, I was in a hurry."

"By now the whole restaurant probably knows you have plans for later — but I don't understand why we're in such a hurry."

"You will. But I would suggest a nap for now," I instruct as I pull out of the parking lot.

"Why?" Jordan asks with her eyes wide.

I wink at her. "Naughty plans and all that —"

"You're such a tease," Jordan crosses her arms in front of her. "You've been gone a long time. I'm totally down with naughty plans."

"Rest up, it'll take me a bit to get to where we're going. You've had a lot of stuff to handle today, so you might as well sleep while you can."

Jordan stifles a yawn. "Oh great! Did you have to mention being tired? I didn't get much sleep while you were gone and I'm exhausted. I didn't notice it so much — until you pointed it out."

"Well, I didn't sleep any better than you did. It's hard to be apart."

Jordan shrugs out of her jacket and balls it up and puts it behind her head. "You were probably joking, but

I'll take you up on the offer of a nap."

"Go right ahead. I have had way too much coffee today. I may not sleep for the next two weeks," I joke.

"Since you're driving, I'd rather you not sleep," Jordan retorts as she closes her eyes. "Wake me up when we're there."

A while later, I slow down to a crawl so I can tackle the gravel drive, which leads to our destination. The change of pace wakes Jordan up. Groggily she sits up and says, "Where are we?" As she looks around, she asks, "Are you taking me four wheeling? Isn't it a little late?"

I'm squirming with excitement as I try to sound casual. "Well, we're not going four-wheeling today, but soon you'll have the option to do it whenever you want to."

Every time I drive up this road, I fall in love a little more. There are huge Douglas fir trees on either side of the drive. As I pull into the circular drive, the house gleams white with its impressive wraparound porch and columns.

"Oh … pretty! Are we staying at this bed-and-breakfast?" Jordan asks as she takes in the scene before her.

I smile as I grasp her hand. "Jordan, how do you feel about staying in a place like this for the rest of our lives?"

Her jaw is slack for a moment. "Do you mean what I think you mean?"

"Wait until you see it. It's like the first owners designed it specifically for us."

"This is why you bought pie?"

"Well, every celebration needs dessert, right? Banana cream pie happens to be my favorite. They didn't have chess pie, so, I hope you like it."

"I love banana cream pie — but it seems like we might have other more pressing things to talk about. Why did you buy a house without me being part of the decision?"

I shrug. "My attorney pointed this out. I saw a video tour of it and instantly fell in love. I knew a house like this wouldn't sit on the market long, so I jumped. Do you hate it? I know you despise my condo in Aspen. I figured you might like this better."

"Wait … you bought this house sight unseen? Geez, I thought I was impulsive. You make me look like an amateur. Why didn't you have me come check it out for you?"

"If I had done that, I wouldn't be able to surprise you. I'm wondering if this was a good idea after all. I expected you to be a little more excited. This is an epic house."

Jordan glances over at me as she bites her lip. "I didn't say I don't like it, I'm just trying to come to grips with the fact that you purchased a house you hadn't even seen. That's huge!"

"I've seen the house a couple times since I purchased it. I was waiting for the paperwork to clear the bank. I wanted to make sure I owned it before I showed it to you. Speaking of huge, you won't believe everything in this house."

Jordan reaches back and puts the pie on the backseat. She opens her door. "Show me what you bought —"

I open my door and sprint around the car to help her out. "Okay, let me tell you about the outside. We own five acres, but it backs up to BLM land. So, you can go four wheeling anytime you want to. There is plenty of room for a big dog to run around."

Jordan takes a deep breath. "The smell is absolutely incredible."

"That's fresh air. We are going to breathe it every single day. Isn't it great?" I practically dance in circles around her as we walk toward the front door.

Jordan arches her eyebrow as she teases, "Excited much? There's air everywhere around us."

I blush a little. "But it's not this air!"

Jordan takes a deep breath again as she comments, "Okay, you have a point. It's really great out here. Can you imagine what it'll look like if we have snow? It'll be like a Christmas-themed postcard."

I grab her belt loop and steer her toward the front door. "Look at this door! Mr. Potter carved this himself."

Jordan runs her fingers across the intricately carved landscape on the door. "This is remarkable. Is there more of this kind of thing in the house?"

"There is. I persuaded them to sell me their headboard Mr. Potter made. He was quite shrewd. He knew I wanted it, and he charged me a pretty penny — but after you see it, you'll understand why it was worth it."

As soon as I open the door, Jordan gasps. "I don't even know where to look — this looks like something from a magazine. Look at that fireplace!" She spins around. "Oh, my gosh! Those are granite countertops. This is amazing. Did you see the kitchen actually has two ovens and a dishwasher? My mom will have to come over and show me some more of her recipes. She would get a kick out of this kitchen — it looks like the ones they use on the cooking shows on TV."

"Yeah, it's the first thing I thought of when I saw this place. Can you imagine how great it'll be to get both of our families together for holidays like Thanksgiving or Christmas? This is the perfect space for it."

"What if your family hates me? I can take a little getting used to," Jordan frets.

"My family won't hate you because I love you. The fact that you love me will win my mother over like a full card at the bingo hall."

"Show me the rest, please."

"I should probably save this until last for dramatic effect, but I don't have the patience to wait. I want to know what you think." I lace my fingers through hers and walk her through the great room and down the hall. "This room clinched the sale for me."

I let go of her hand and move behind Jordan. I pull her back into my chest as I say, "Cover your eyes. I want you to get the full effect of this."

Jordan's snickers at me, but closes her eyes. "Okay, whatever you say — it's your surprise."

I reach around her and push open the door. I gently

escort her to the center of the room and then declare, "Jordan, welcome to your new sewing workshop."

Watching the joy fill her face as she looks around the room with its polished wooden floors and big open bay windows is enough to wipe away my fears.

When she spots the item in the corner, she gasps. "Do you see the antique loom? I wish I knew how to operate one. I only know how to use the material after it's been made. Man, oh man! It would be fun to learn how to make my own fabric."

"Before Mrs. Potter's health declined, she used to weave. When Mr. Potter found out you work in textiles, he insisted the loom stay here with someone who loves fabrics as much as his wife. The whole house is set up so her business could operate from home. See the door over there? That door goes to a side porch entrance to this room. So, if you wanted to, you could operate your business from here. Of course, I didn't know you would get an offer from another company. That might change things."

"Oh, I hope not. This space is absolutely perfect. See, I can put my cutting table over there and my dress forms in the bay windows. This space is big enough for me to add a quilting machine if I wanted to."

"We can come back to this room later, but I want to show you some other stuff."

"I can't wait to see! So far, everything you've shown me has been mind-blowing."

"I hope you don't mind having me around, because the Potters have made it possible for us to have his and her studios," I tease as I open the door to yet another large room.

"Is that soundproofing on the walls?" Jordan asks as she examines the odd surface on the walls and ceiling of the room.

"It is! How cool is that? Mr. Potter was a huge ham radio enthusiast, and so he used to broadcast from this room. He claims the noise from the loom drove him crazy, so he added all the soundproofing. It'll be perfect for me to do podcasts or voiceover work in here. I have seen professional studios not as decked out as this room."

"Is there anything in this house I won't like?" Jordan asks as she stands in the middle the room and looks around.

"The only thing I can think of is you might not be fond of the wallpaper in the guest bathroom. It's a little dated, but other than that, we should be all set. Let me show you the back patio."

I walk Jordan back downstairs as I open the back door overlooking the raised patio.

Jordan squeaks with delight as she asks, "Is that a barn over there? Do you mean I can actually have horses here?"

"You probably can't have as many as Madison and Trevor, but I bet you could have a couple. I think the Potters kept a couple of horses for their grandkids."

"Wow! It's like you could see my ideal house through my eyes. This couldn't be more spot-on."

I reach for Jordan's hand as I gently lead her out of the room. "Come with me, I want to show you this house through my eyes." I walk toward a huge bay window next to the kitchen. It overlooks a small meadow beside the house. "Let me tell you what I see. I envision you sitting at this table chewing on the end of your glasses as you try to solve the New York Times crossword puzzle. I'm probably reading some racing magazine while we drink our coffee together. You look up at me and smile as you mention the weather and tell me to be careful when I go to the grocery store."

Jordan looks up at me with a tearful smile as she whispers, "Sounds perfect to me."

I have to swallow hard before I continue, "I know it sounds simple, but I want us to be like the boring, stable couples who celebrate our fiftieth wedding anniversary with the great-grandkids in the back yard. I've done the New York thing and the Los Angeles thing. I don't care for either of those."

"You know how I feel about New York," Jordan says with a grim smile.

"I've always wanted a partner who supports my dreams. I never thought I would find one, but I have found it in you in ways I never expected. You're strong, smart and kind. You don't try to hold me back because my job might make you feel a bit uneasy. Instead, you give me a wonderful welcome every time I come home. You are everything I didn't know I wanted but everything I need. I'd like you by my side for the rest of my life. Are you in?"

Jordan nods mutely as tears roll down her face. Eventually, she finds her words, "I want to share the good life with you — more than anything." She swallows hard and wipes her tears away with the back of her hand.

I place a tender kiss on her forehead.

She buries her face in my neck and then pulls away. "When you saw my life blow up in the middle of Mishka's shop that day, I wanted to die of embarrassment. I had no idea all that drama would lead me to the thing I needed the most. It's ironic that one of the most painful things I've been through made me brave enough to pursue my own path not taken. I never dreamed I could love someone as much as I love you. I still pinch myself every time you tell me you love me … and now I'm going to marry you—" she trails off before she walks into my arms.

We stand there for a moment, just absorbing the memories. "As much as I dislike your former boss, I am so glad she threw you in the middle of my path. My life will never be the same — and that's a very good thing."

After a few seconds, she adds, "I don't know about you, but I think this celebration calls for a bit more than pie."

I reach into my jacket pocket. "You mean a little something like this?" I ask as I pull out a diamond solitaire ring. I take her hand in mine as I start to slide the ring on her finger. "Jordan Shepherd, I love you. Will you be by my side as we forge our paths together in life?"

Jordan moves her hand closer to the ring as she proclaims, "Every step of the way."

Epilogue

Jordan

As we make our way down the red carpet, I can't believe how far we've come in a little more than two years.

Aisha squeals when she sees us. "Oh, my gosh, I thought you guys were on a shoot in the middle of nowhere and not able to come to this. I was so bummed. It's a major accomplishment for *Razors Edge* to be up for an award even though it's a brand-new show. I didn't want Cristiano to miss it."

I hug my friend quickly. "I didn't want him to miss out on being honored either, so that's why I adjusted our travel plans a bit so we could make this event. Can you believe you and I have been friends for this long already?"

Aisha laughs. "I believe it. I see evidence of it every time I open my closet. I am the best-dressed reporter in all the nation. Trust me, I know these things."

Aisha studies me from head to toe. "Did you just whip something up for this event?"

I cringe a bit as I admit, "I did. Just don't tell

Cristiano how much the fabric cost."

When Aisha sees my hand, she sucks in a breath. "What is this? This is not the same ring you had the last time we had lunch. What gives?"

I blushed deeply. "Well, we might have gotten married the last time Cristiano covered a race in Las Vegas."

"And you didn't invite me?" Aisha protests.

"Well, it was kind of one of those spur-of-the-moment things. We decided to do it on the anniversary of the day we met. It was one of those completely cheesy drive-through ceremony places — but it didn't matter to us because we were having so much fun."

"What does your mom think?"

"We may have forgotten to tell everyone but you. Most people aren't quite as observant as you are. We haven't made a secret of our marriage because I wear my ring all the time. However, most people still believe Cristiano and I are just engaged."

"I know you're my friend and everything, but I have to say you guys are a little weird," Aisha responds as she inspects my ring. "Although, I do have to say Cristiano has exquisite taste in wedding rings. I think it makes the perfect accessory to your outfit."

Someone bumps me from behind, and I am thrown forward on my high heels. Cristiano has to reach out and catch me to prevent me from falling. As I look behind me, it's almost as if my past has come back to slap me in the face. I growl in frustration. I can't even enjoy my husband's accomplishments without my history hanging over my head.

"Mishka, good to see you." I try to make my voice even and pleasant. Minding my manners, I stick my hand out for her to shake.

Mishka bats it away. "Oh, if it isn't the traitor," she snaps as she frowns at me. "It's a little ironic that suddenly you have all this talent to become a media darling, yet you couldn't do that when you worked for me. Why is that? Were you holding back on me?"

Cristiano steps up and puts his arm around my waist. "Please don't insult my wife. I was in the room when you told me Jordan would never be talented enough to be a designer for you. You told me you wouldn't hire her. I'm sorry you feel differently now, but that's not Jordan's problem."

"Problem? Jordan doesn't know the meaning of the word problem. Her actions have caused me to become a laughing stock in the design community. I can't get a job in any design house in this whole city. It doesn't matter whether I'm on the West Coast or the East Coast. Everyone hates me."

"It's funny how that works. When you steal other people's work and claim it as your own, no one feels comfortable working for you," I say blandly.

"No one can prove I did that, I was very careful to cover my tracks," Mishka blurts.

Aisha nods at her cameraman. "Apparently, you didn't cover them carefully enough. I would advise you to leave Jordan out of your mess. She has no intention of going back. Just a word to the wise, it's not usually advisable to admit to intellectual theft on national TV."

"What do you mean?" Mishka asks dramatically as she covers her chest with her hand.

"Don't tell me you haven't been around cameras during your fashion shoots?" Cristiano challenges.

"Why of course I have," she answers quickly "I am a professional after all."

I raise my eyebrow. "All evidence to the contrary."

"You don't know what I did for your career. Jordan Shepherd wouldn't exist if it weren't for me. I have the power to destroy you. Surely, you know that."

I glance up at the cameras which are producing the live feed for *Are You Gonna Wear That?!* It appears they're not currently running. I guide Mishka over to a more private corner and sit down because my heels are killing me.

After I perch on the tall bar stool, I examine my former boss. She hardly resembles the woman I first met after I graduated from college.

"Okay, you got me in a nice private spot. How about you come at me with a settlement figure I can live with?"

I shake my head vigorously. "No! Why in the world would I settle with you? I haven't done anything wrong. You think you have the power to decimate me, but you don't. Over the past two years, I've discovered your threats simply aren't true. The only person who can destroy me is me. I have chosen to take the best of a terrible situation and turn it into a powerful message."

"You want brownie points for that?" Mishka asks snidely.

"No, actually I don't. My request is more straight forward. I want you to publicly apologize for the things you said about me. You know good and well I never stole any designs."

"I'm aware. Without you around, my whole business fell apart. I had to get noticed in the news. In this business, you are only as good as your last design."

"Speaking of that? When was your last design? Not one you hired someone to do, but one you made with your own hand —"

"You were there in the beginning. I used to do all my own stuff. Then my muse left, and I can't find her. I can't design if I'm not inspired."

"When that happens, you work in collaboration with someone until you work through it. You don't steal other people's work, and you don't accuse people of theft as a publicity stunt."

"I didn't think it was going to be a big deal. Artists who are creative like you make drawings all the time. Sooner or later, I figured people's discarded designs were better than what I was coming up with."

"Why not wish me well and let me go on my way? Why did you have to try to destroy me?"

"Because I knew I'd be nothing without you. You were the one holding Mishka Unlimited together. As soon as you left, I knew it was the beginning of the end. I was livid that you had so much power over me. I hired you as an intern. I never dreamed you would actually be better than me."

"Mishka, I'm sorry things turned out the way they

did. At one point, you were a good friend. However, I've moved on with my life, and I have a whole new career."

I can see Mishka's temple throbbing as she snaps, "What am I supposed to do now?"

"I'm sorry I can't help you. I was loyal to you for years. You didn't take the time to appreciate my work or my talents. I've chosen a different path. Whatever your issues are, you couldn't pay me enough to deal with them. I'm sad it all unfolded this way. From now on, if you need to talk to me, you know my attorney's number."

Mishka turns to Aisha who is hovering in the background, ready to jump in if I need her and says, "Can you see what a rude woman she is? I can't believe I put up with this insolence for so many years."

Aisha glares back. "The only rude person I see here is you. By the way, I have a suggestion. If you are serious about making it to the top, you might work on your own talent instead of tearing others down."

Mishka clutches her chest dramatically. "Well, I never —"

I squeeze Cristiano's hand. "Yeah, a whole lot of things happened this year I never expected." I hold up our clasped hands. "I'd like to thank you for giving me a giant shove to change the direction of my life. I'm glad I followed my heart."

Cristiano places his arm around my waist and helps me get off the tall stool. He escorts me away from Mishka and Aisha as we make our way down the red carpet. By the time I stop to take a breath, my knees are shaking.

"I never expected to discover the love of my life

when I went shopping for a suit. I am so proud of you," Cristiano says with a tender smile. "Way to hold your own."

"Mr. Romero, what do you have to say to your fans?" a reporter shouts. "Are you surprised *The X-Games: Razor's Edge* is up for an award?"

Cristiano smiles for the camera and then pulls me close for a kiss.

After he breaks away, he holds up our clasped hands to the camera as he says, "I'd like to thank all the fans for their support and most of all, my wife, Jordan Shepherd Romero. These days, I've learned not to have expectations. Sometimes, in the race of life, pulling a surprise move or two means the difference between winning or losing."

When my husband bends me over into a theatrical kiss and winks at the camera, several people on the red carpet start to applaud.

As Cristiano helps me stand back up and balance on my impossibly high heels, I catch Aisha's eye. I grin when I hear her announce to her fans, "Ladies and gentlemen, I've had a front row seat during the courtship of Cristiano and Jordan. I'm here to tell you, that's the way to do love right. With those parting words, I'll say good night to the red carpet and go see who wins."

I wasn't expecting an emotional speech from Aisha. I am trying desperately hard not to cry and ruin my beautiful makeup. I take a few deep breaths and swallow hard. I don't even know what to say. I'm still reeling from Cristiano's public announcement of our marriage. I suspect I'll get some grief about that. I haven't told my family yet. I know Cristiano hasn't told his either.

A series of camera flashes temporarily blind me and remind me all of that is a worry for another day. Cristiano notices my odd, preoccupied mood. "Come on Jor, we need to get into our seats before the ceremony starts. If it's meant to be, it will happen. Regardless of what happens tonight, we've already won."

As we move toward the inside of the building, a woman in a wheelchair stops me. "I know we are here to honor your husband, but I just wanted to tell you what a difference you made in my life. Because you did what you did, I now have a sense of dignity I didn't have before. Your clothes are wonderful and exactly what I needed. It almost makes me feel as beautiful as I was before I had my diving accident."

"I didn't know you before your accident, but I think you look stunning now." I dig in my little clutch and pull out a business card. "Contact Matthew or Kalina at this number. They are looking for models for our new winter line. I'm sure they would love to have you star in their ads."

"Wow, that's not something I'd considered, but I think it's a great idea."

"I wish you the best of luck in whatever you decide to do. I'm just glad I was able to help you with your wardrobe dilemmas."

Aisha closes out her shoot and catches up to us. "See? I told you so. What you are doing is far more important than any fame."

"I know. Forming JS Couture and using my skills to help others has led me to everything wonderful in my life."

Aisha scrutinizes Cristiano. "I can't argue with you there. Your man is pretty fantastic. I only hope one day I find someone like him."

"You never know, you could be in the middle of a meltdown with your boss and quit your job," I quip.

"I don't think that's a strategy for everyone, but it seemed to work great for you."

"It did at that," I retort as I lace my fingers through Cristiano's. "Aisha, don't lose faith, you never know where your path is going to take you," I say gently.

"You think so?" Aisha asks with hope in her eyes.

"We are sure of it," Cristiano answers as he brings my hand to his lips and kisses it. "Some of the best things in life aren't planned."

THE END

The next book in the Hidden Beauty Series is Heart Wish. It is available now.

Dear Reader:

Thank you so much for reading *Paths Not Taken*. I hope you enjoyed it. The next book in the series is *Heart Wish*.

You'll meet new friends and catch up with old ones in this crossover book. This contemporary romance novel includes characters from both series. Best of all, 100% of the net profits will go to ChildFind.

"If you do one good deed your reward usually is to be set to do another and harder and better one."
— C. S. Lewis, *The Horse and His Boy*.

As an avid book reader, Kendall Kordes lives by the C. S. Lewis quote.

Her days are filled with the highest of highs and lowest of lows.

As much as she loves her job at Locate My Heart, an agency which helps find children, for personal reasons, it's difficult.

Her life becomes even more difficult when a ransomware attack strikes locate My Heart.

To make matters worse, the technician sent to fix the problem seems to hate her.

Jameson Payne feels justified in disliking everything Kendall and her agency stand for. But, to explain his attitude, he must face some hard truths.

Can Jameson and Kendall reconcile their pasts so they can move forward?

Love should be more than just a heart wish.

You'll love this emotionally wrenching story of love lost and hope found.

Get *Heart Wish* in paperback, as an e-book, or for free through Kindle Unlimited now.

~Mary

Paths Not Taken

Because love matters, differences don't.

ACKNOWLEDGEMENTS

At heart, I am an advocate. Most specifically, I am an advocate for diversity and acceptance. Last year, I was participating in a discussion on a writing board, and someone asked a very simple question. I am paraphrasing here — but the conversation went a little something like this, "In every romance I ever read, happily ever after is always defined as getting married and having children. Don't these authors know it is possible to have a happily ever after without children?"

Anybody who knows me, probably can guess that I accepted the story premise as a challenge. After all, valuing diversity means you honor it across the board — even if the person making the choice would make a different decision than you would. Out of that discussion, Paths Not Taken was born. I hope I adequately gave a voice to the couples who decide for whatever reason not to have children. Families come in all shapes and sizes. It is not our place to question how someone else chooses to live their life. It is the differences between us which makes life interesting.

I would like to take this moment to highlight how much I appreciate the author community, especially other indie authors, formatters, designers and social media consultants. Without your assistance, my books would suffer greatly. I will make every effort to pay your help forward.

As always, thank you to Kathern Watts. Your unfailing support keeps me organized and writing.

A special shout-out to my beta readers. Thanks, guys. This was a tough one.

About the Author

I have been lucky enough to live my own version of a romance novel. I married the guy who kissed me at summer camp. He told me on the night we met that he was going to marry me and be the father of my children.

Eventually, I stopped giggling when he said it, and we've been married for over thirty years. We have two children. The oldest is a Doctor of Osteopathy. He is across the United States completing his residency, but when he's done, he is going to come back to Oregon and practice Family Medicine. Our youngest son is now tackling high school, where he is an honor student. He is interested in becoming an EMT.

I write full time now. I have published more than thirty books and have several more underway. I volunteer my time to a variety of causes. I have worked as a Civil Rights Attorney and diversity advocate. I spent several years working for various social service agencies before becoming an attorney.

In my spare time, I love to cook, decorate cakes and, of course, I obsessively, compulsively read.

I would be honored if you would take a few moments out of your busy day to check out my website, MaryCrawfordAuthor.com. While you're there, you can sign up for my newsletter and get a free book. I will be announcing my upcoming books and giving sneak peeks as well as sponsoring giveaways and giving you information about other interesting events.

If you have questions or comments, please E-mail me at Mary@MaryCrawfordAuthor.com or find me on the following social networks:

Facebook: www.facebook.com/authormarycrawford

Website: MaryCrawfordAuthor.com

Twitter: www.twitter.com/MaryCrawfordAut